CHRISTINA
AND THE
REBEL AFFAIR

Novel #6

R. LINDA

CHRISTINA AND THE REBEL AFFAIR

Copyright © 2018 by R. Linda.
All rights reserved.
First Print Edition: October 2018

Limitless Publishing, LLC
Kailua, HI 96734
www.limitlesspublishing.com

Formatting: Limitless Publishing

ISBN-13: 978-1-64034-443-3
ISBN-10: 1-64034-443-8

DEDICATION

To Trent

For your constant support and interest in my writing, even if you'll probably never read a book because they sound like me.

I love you x

CHAPTER ONE

I should have kicked him out last night, told him he couldn't stay and to go home. But who was I kidding? I could never say no to that man. I leaned against the doorframe and watched him as he stepped out of my shower, water dripping down that firm chest my fingers ached to touch.

"You could have joined me, you know?" he said, wrapping the towel around his waist and coming to stand in front of me.

"And you know we'd never get out, and then I'd be late for work." I leaned into him, standing on the tips of my toes to kiss him. I couldn't understand how he still gave me butterflies, made my heart stutter in my chest and my palms sweat. I didn't know I could feel like that with another person.

My last boyfriend was boring, safe, and predictable. He was an accountant and enjoyed watching documentaries way too much. I'd stayed with him for over a year because he didn't manipulate me or cause me any pain, like my previous boyfriend—the man I believed was the love of my life. But this man in front of me was different than any other. He was fun and outgoing and made me feel things I didn't know were possible. Granted, we didn't talk a lot, and spent most of our time in my bed, yet he still made me giddy.

"I'd be okay with that." He wrapped his arms around my waist and kissed me hard, making me want to drag him back to bed and make use of the silk scarf I'd bought the day I met him.

I sighed into his mouth as his fingers danced along my spine, and I gave in, dragging him back to my rumpled bed.

He grinned. "Knew you'd see sense."

***

I really was going to be late now, but it was totally worth it. Once my house was empty and I was alone, I hurried to get ready. It was my first day at my new job, and to say I was nervous would be an understatement. I was heading back to my hometown after not stepping foot in the place for years. But it was time to face my fears—and the people I'd hurt during my time there.

I walked into the office with trepidation and was greeted by John Sawyer. He was an old friend of my father's and offered me the job when he'd heard I was looking for work. It couldn't have come at a better time. We chatted for a few minutes about what he expected of me before he showed me around the school. It wasn't like I didn't know my way around. I'd spent five years in the place, but I humoured him and let him give me the tour. We finally arrived at the class I was taking over in a week's time.

"Now, Ms. Mitchell is one of our best teachers, and we're sad to see her leave so soon," he said. My ears pricked up at the name of the teacher. I wondered whether it could be her. How many other Mitchells were around? But I figured she'd have been married and would be a Jones by now. "She's very thorough and well organised and will have you up to speed in no time." He opened the door and politely interrupted the class to introduce me.

I walked in behind him, my stomach churning from nerves, and my heart stopped. It was her. Principal Sawyer introduced me then left me to face Bailey alone.

She looked great. Pregnancy suited her, but the look she gave me made me realise she'd still not forgiven me for the way I treated her years ago. I'd grown up a lot since then, changed, and it was all because of Chace. Schooling my expression into something neutral, I turned and smiled at the class, noticing the cosy couple in the back corner.

"Can I see you outside?" Bailey asked quietly, smoothing her hands over her protruding stomach and indicating the door with her head.

I turned and walked back out into the hall. Bailey spoke to the class and gave them some work to do for a few minutes while I waited. I watched through the door as the students got themselves organised, except for the young couple in the back corner. They were huddled together, his head pressed into her shoulder as they whispered. The girl's eyes met

3

mine and widened briefly. I thought I saw a flash of recognition in them but didn't know why. I'd never seen her before. She spoke urgently to her boyfriend. He groaned in frustration and straightened, pulling the ball cap off his head and running his fingers through his long golden hair, and then he looked over his shoulder at me and smirked.

Oh, my god.

Bennett.

I stared at him, shock holding me still as he refused to break eye contact until Bailey walked out the door.

"Bennett, Audrey, get moving," she said, closing the door behind her.

She faced me, her arms crossed over the top of her belly, and raised an eyebrow. "What are you doing here, Christina?"

"I'm your replacement," I said, unable to help the sarcasm in my voice, my eyes still on Bennett's through the window. "Thought Principal Sawyer made that obvious."

Bailey frowned. "How long have you been back?"

"A few months. I live in Storm Cove, not here," I said, still distracted by Bennett. He was talking to the girl, his hand squeezing hers. I swallowed the lump in my throat.

I'd moved back a few months ago, but decided Blackhill wasn't for me anymore. I wanted to stay away from the drama and the small-minded town I grew up in. Unfortunately, the plans I had after university fell through, and I had no choice but to come back.

"What do you want?"

"To work. Same as everyone else." I inspected my nails, already bored with the conversation and wanting to look at anything but the girl who was leaning against Bennett like her life depended on it.

I understood Bailey's hesitance toward me. I had treated her like crap in our last year of school, and even worse throughout university, but if I was being honest, I had been blinded by Chace. Once I realised the type of person he was, the way he manipulated people into thinking and believing whatever he wanted them to, I tried to distance myself from him and everyone in his path as much as possible. I'd transferred out of uni to a different school about a year after I started, and worked hard to be a better person. I hadn't seen Bailey or spoken to her for a couple of years, if not more.

"I don't want any trouble, Christina. I'm finally happy and settled with Ryder. Life is great. I don't want you walking back into my life and destroying it again."

"I'm not here for that. I just want to teach." I held my hands up defensively and thought about apologising but knew she wouldn't accept it. It was far too late. There was too much water under the bridge.

"Right."

"I'm not here for you, Bailey. My life doesn't revolve around making you miserable."

Bailey let out a disbelieving laugh.

"Not anymore. I'm here because there was work."

"I hope you're right." She looked back over her shoulder into the classroom. Bennett and the girl, Audrey—was she his girlfriend?—were still staring at us. "These are good kids, Christina. They deserve the best. I don't want you coming in and tainting their lives."

It might have been too late, but I couldn't tell her that. I couldn't tell her I'd had a fling with someone, and if anyone found out, it would end my career and destroy both our lives. She already thought I was the worst person alive, and maybe she was right.

"Look, a lot has happened. We've grown up, moved on, and made our own lives. I have no interest in yours, or the students'. I'm here to teach, and that's it," I said.

"Well, I guess you better come in, then, and I'll get you all caught up." She pushed open the door and gestured for me to head back into the classroom full of students, including the one I'd had a fling with.

CHAPTER TWO

Bennett

Audrey tensed beside me the moment Ms. M. asked the replacement teacher outside, though it could have been the fact I buried my head in her chest to hide from the very same teacher.

Gut reaction.

What was I supposed to do?

"Bro?" I asked, reaching for her hand under the table and rubbing soothing circles on her skin to calm her rapid breathing before she had a panic attack.

"Do you know who that is?" she whispered in my ear and glanced over my shoulder at the door.

"Oh, yeah. I know who that is," I said into her shoulder with a groan.

"That's Christina."

Yep. Knew that. Quite well.

"The same Christina who slept with Bailey's high school boyfriend," she said.

I lifted my eyebrows. I didn't know that.

7

"Interesting." I adjusted the hat on my head and tried to covertly sneak a peek at the chick I knew so well in so many different ways. Positions.

I stared through the small window in the classroom door, my eyes trained on Christina as she tried to focus on what Ms. M. was saying and not on me. She was just as shocked to see me sitting in this class as I was to watch her walk in there with my father. She stood tall, spoke to Bailey, and flicked her eyes back to me every so often. Her long blonde hair that I had tangled in my fist not two hours earlier was pulled back in a sleek bun. Her clothes, a cross between a preppy country club member and a librarian—hot as hell—were a stark contrast to the simple jeans and t-shirts I was used to seeing her in.

She was dressed for her first day at her new job.

And the kicker…

She was a fucking teacher.

I smirked.

Shit.

I was fucking my teacher.

I threw my head back and laughed.

"What's so funny?" Audrey hissed beside me.

"Everything." I bit my lip to stop laughing after one look from her. She wasn't impressed.

"Bennett?"

I leaned in close. "That chick I've been seeing?"

Audrey nodded and pinched her eyebrows together, something she did when she was concentrating or trying to focus.

"Ms. Brown." I couldn't help it; I smiled and laughed again. The whole situation was hilarious.

What were the chances I'd hook up with my teacher?

"What?" Audrey screeched.

I covered her mouth with my hand. "Shhh."

"Tell me you're joking." She gripped my hand tight under the table, her fingernails digging into my palm.

I didn't say anything.

"Bennett. You're joking, right?" Her voice was higher than usual. "Please tell me you're joking?"

Still, I didn't say anything.

"Why aren't you answering me?"

"You know I can't lie to you." I shrugged. If I couldn't lie to her, it was better to not say anything.

Audrey whimpered. Sounded like a puppy. Her eyes widened, and she looked over my shoulder. I turned my head. Bailey and Christina were coming back in. Bailey looked annoyed, and Christina appeared amused, until her eyes drifted over me. Then her lips puckered and her eyebrow creased.

"This discussion isn't over," Audrey said softly and faced the front of the class, keeping her head low and her face covered by her hair.

"Sorry about that, everyone," Bailey announced once she was behind her desk again. "Just had to have a chat with Ms. Brown about where you're all up to in the coursework and the preparations that need to be made to ensure your exams go as smoothly as possible."

Ms. Brown. I liked the sound of that. I muffled another laugh as I wondered—

"Something funny, Bennett? Would you like to share?" Bailey called across the classroom with an eyebrow raised.

I shook my head and bit my lip as I reached for the pen on my desk. Anything to distract me from the woman sitting in the corner of the room watching me.

"What is wrong with you?" Audrey elbowed me in the ribs when Bailey turned around. "Get it together."

"I'm trying, bro. But—"

"No. No buts."

"Just wondering whether she'd let me call her Ms. Brown in bed."

"Oh, my god, Bennett. Focus." Audrey pushed some papers in front of me. Revision notes and suggested reading materials for the exam.

I stared at the sheets for a few minutes, not taking anything in. My eyes kept drifting to Christina. Ms. Brown. Wondering what would happen next.

Would she hate me for not telling her I was a student?

Or...

Would she like it, like some forbidden fetish or something?

I was hoping for the latter.

"Put that phone away," Audrey scolded me and reached under the table to snatch my phone from my hand. I hadn't realised I had dug it out of my pocket.

"Give it back."

As if knowing I was planning on sending a text to the sexy new English teacher, Audrey scoffed and slid the phone inside her top. Ha, like that would stop me from trying to get it back. As long as her boyfriend Brody didn't find out I "accidentally" felt her up at the same time. I was still afraid that dude would kill me and cover it up one of these days. I figured working in the medical field had its advantages, and he could probably murder me and make it appear as though I died of natural causes.

She raised an eyebrow. "No."

I lifted my hand, preparing to dive under her shirt and get my phone back, when she tilted her head and looked at Christina. I sighed and followed her gaze. I was met with an icy cold stare that pierced my chest and made my skin erupt in goose bumps.

So, I did what any man would do in my situation.

I winked.

At Christina.

I made a show of dragging my eyes over her body, just so she'd know where I stood.

And then I turned back to my papers and began to study.

***

"Okay, spill," Audrey said the moment I met her outside under the tree in the corner of the courtyard, where we ate lunch away from the watchful eyes of the rest of the student body. Really, though, it wasn't as bad as she believed it to be. Most of the students barely even looked at her these days. They all knew her story, and they all moved on. But she was still convinced everyone looked at her and judged her.

11

I sat beside her and snatched her chocolate milk, taking a big sip as she frowned at me. "There's not much to tell."

"You're sleeping with a teacher, Bennett. How could you be so stupid?" She slapped my chest with the back of her hand.

"I didn't know she was a teacher, and she didn't know I was a student." I took a bite of my burger before handing it to Audrey.

She still didn't eat a lot, a symptom of her anxiety. But it didn't take me too long to realise she'd eat my food if I told her I couldn't finish it. And that was precisely what I did. Every day. I'd buy two lunches, quickly eat one, then take the other to her and claim I wasn't hungry.

"How could you not know?" She stared at me, her mouth hanging open.

"Didn't come up in conversation." I shrugged and leaned forward to close her mouth before that bite of burger she'd taken fell out.

"Dude, asking someone what they do for a living is like Getting to Know a Person 101. It always comes up in conversation."

"Not if you skip the getting to know you part and get straight to the best part…"

She lifted an eyebrow and crossed her arms over her chest, dropping the burger into its wrapper on the grass where it stayed, forgotten.

"Getting naked."

"Seriously?" She groaned and wiggled, shaking her chest from side to side, a small frown pinching her eyebrows. I was not ashamed to admit I openly stared. I mean, what guy would look away when a

12

chick with a killer rack shook them in his face? What was she doing?

She pulled her shirt out and looked down her top before reaching inside and taking my phone out. Huh, I forgot she had that. She threw it at me. "You don't talk to each other?" she continued as though she hadn't just given me an image to dream about tonight.

"Not really."

I met Christina over the break. We chatted about trivial stuff, the weather, whatever. Went out for a couple of drinks and ended up back at her place. She told me she was looking for work after moving to town. I told her I worked at the surf shop. It wasn't a lie. I did work there. Only it was more a seasonal thing. Or whenever dad pissed me off enough that I begged for shifts just to get out of the house.

"How is that even possible? Who gets naked with someone they don't even know?"

Someone who needed a distraction.

A person trying to move on. Get over an ex…or lost love. A person who constantly questioned "what if…?"

"Me." I grinned at her.

She rolled her eyes.

"Did you miss our conversation this morning about nipple clamps?"

Christina was kinky enough to provide the perfect distraction, at least for the time I spent with her. During that time, my mind was so out of it that I couldn't even remember my own name. But…when I was alone, nothing could distract me

13

enough, and all I could think was I just needed an extra twelve months, and everything would have fallen into place. Everything would have been perfect. Mine. Right.

"Oh, my god. I don't want to hear any more." She covered her eyes. She was so easy to torment.

"Nipple clamps, Audrey. Can you blame me for not wanting to talk so we can get straight to the good stuff?"

"Stop. Please."

Even with a boyfriend seven years older, she was still so innocent and naïve. I loved embarrassing her. She got this cute little flush to her cheeks, and her eyes fluttered closed as she looked down at her feet.

"What? I'm just trying to give you ideas. Maybe you want some suggestions for you and Brody." I laughed, tilting her chin up to look at me.

She pushed my hand away. "We don't need ideas, thank you very much."

"Really? Do tell." I leaned forward and stared into her dark brown eyes, urging her to answer me and secretly hoping she wouldn't. I really didn't want the dirty details of what went on in her room after we ended our nightly video chats.

"A lady never tells." She pursed her lips and lifted her nose in the air, faking a British accent.

"Prude."

"Slut."

"I take offence, bro." I clutched my chest as though I was in pain.

Audrey shrugged. "You're the one sleeping with your teacher."

14

"And you're in a relationship with the guy who saved your life, who is also related to the family taking care of you. You're practically brother and sister."

"Gross, Bennett. Don't twist things into something they're not. You know damn well we're not related. And—" She was cut off by the bell ringing.

"Well, as much as I'd love to continue this interesting conversation, we have class. Let's go, cupcake." I stood and reached down to her. Pulling her to her feet, I grabbed both our bags and threw my arm over her shoulder and escorted her to her locker.

The kids at this school sucked. All of them. They were obnoxious. Rude. Cruel. And they didn't have a compassionate bone in their bodies. Except maybe for Lucy, the tiny blonde in our art class. She was sweet.

I hated the thought of leaving Audrey alone for a moment in this place. She'd get eaten by the wolves. And as hard as I tried to get my class schedule changed to be with her, my father wouldn't let me.

"Don't destroy your life over some broad," he said. But it was Audrey, and she wasn't some broad. She was the best person I knew. My best friend. My bro. Her strength and courage were an inspiration, and I hated leaving her to fend for herself.

The scars she carried, both physical and emotional, were what made her so special. She'd lived through a tragedy, been through more than most people would ever have to suffer in their lives, and she came out the other side intact.

The guys were dicks, and the chicks were bitches. Many of them never failed to point out that Audrey looked different, but not all of them. Most would just ignore her, which in my opinion was just as bad as ridiculing her. Still, no one ever stood up for her or reached out to speak to her unless they absolutely had to.

It had been the two of us since day one when we bonded over our mutual disdain for returning to school. And it would always be the two of us. I looked out for her every chance I got, and no one messed with me. Perks of being the six-feet, four-inch son of the principal.

We swung by her locker, ignoring the crowds milling around us, and grabbed her books before heading to mine. The chatter was incessant. Rumours circulated and recirculated at this school faster than Tiffany got around the football team, and the current story was about Audrey and me once again.

It wasn't a particularly original rumour. Everyone assumed we were dating because we were always together—she was my bro—and no one could understand why I would be dating her. Sometimes I dispelled the rumours, sometimes I encouraged them.

They thought she was disfigured. Weird. A freak. And I knew if any of them bothered to get to know her the way I had, they'd love her as much as I did.

I walked Audrey to class, handed her books over, and dropped a kiss to the top of her head.

"Shoulders," I said as I placed my hands on her shoulders and pushed them back. Audrey sighed.

If she pushed her shoulders back, she stood taller and looked less intimidated.

"Head," I reminded her and pinched her chin between my thumb and forefinger so I could tilt it up, only for her to roll her eyes.

If she held her head high, she'd appear confident.

"Ignore?"

"The losers," Audrey said, a small smile on her face.

"Why?"

"Because you're the only friend I need." Her lips pulled into a cheesy grin as she repeated my poor pep talk back to me, but it worked. She always walked away from me with a smile. As long as I made her smile, I was happy.

"And don't you forget it, bro." I reached out a fist to bump against hers. "I'll see you after school."

Audrey shook her head. "It's Brody's day."

Brody. Her hero. Her older, paramedic boyfriend. He worked crazy shifts but liked to pick her up from school as often as he possibly could, sometimes even going so far as to get his shift swapped. They were goofy in love. I internally cringed at the thought, but I couldn't blame them. He saved her life. They bonded. And they lived in the same house. Things were bound to happen.

It was my turn to shake my head. "I'll see you after school. Right here."

"Bennett."

"Nope, don't argue. I'll be here." Like I was every day.

17

"Wasn't arguing. Just pointing out that I won't be here after school. I have social studies next period and will be there. Not here." She wrinkled her nose and tried not to laugh.

"Fine. I'll be there, then."

"Thank you."

I turned her around and gave her a gentle shove toward the door, but not before tapping her ass lightly. Brody would kill me for it if he knew, but I didn't care, and Audrey did what she always did, ignored it.

CHAPTER THREE

Christina

I'd tried to subtly ask Bailey who the girl with Bennett was this morning without giving away that I knew Bennett more than I should. Other than telling me she was quiet and kept to herself and that I should go easy on her because she'd had a rough time, she wouldn't give me much information. That was it. It didn't help to ease the heavy feeling in my stomach. I was so screwed.

I'd spent two blissful weeks with a guy who knew his way around the bedroom. The kitchen. The bathroom. Back seat of my car.

A guy who turned out to be my student.

A guy who might possibly have a girlfriend.

A guy who, regardless of those last two points, I wanted to see again.

I'd watched him during lunch from the other side of the courtyard as he sat with her. The quiet girl, Audrey. I'd watched him share his food with her. Laugh with her. Even from where I sat in the

19

teacher's lounge, I could see the way his eyes lit up when she spoke to him.

What did she have that I didn't? His eyes never sparkled like that when he looked at me.

I had just about convinced myself that they were friends and nothing more until I saw him wrap his arm around her and walk her to class. I knew this because, like a dog with a bone, I wasn't one to give up, so I followed. Right from her locker, to his, to her next class, they walked with his arm around her. He even carried her books.

What high school guy carried a girl's books if he wasn't trying to get up her skirt, or stay there? The only time my high school disaster Chace ever carried my books was when I let him feel me up in the janitor's closet.

He kissed her head. Not really the passionate type of kiss he'd given me earlier that morning, but there was something sweet and protective about it. Powerful. Dominating. It was as though he was marking his territory and telling anyone around them that she belonged to him. It was exactly the way I remembered seeing Ryder with Bailey when they started dating. Ownership.

And then he straightened her back, grasped her chin, his eyes blazing to life when she smiled up at him with all the adoration in the world.

I swallowed the bitterness in my throat.

She wasn't anything special, from what I could tell.

Then they fist bumped.

And I was confused again. Fist bumps were reserved for friends. Not lovers. But the kiss on her head and the book carrying, that was something for couples.

My head was spinning as I moved out of my hiding spot and walked past her classroom. Bennett had gone in the other direction, so I glanced inside to see her sitting alone in the back corner, head down, hair covering her face, shoulders slumped. She was a stark contrast to the girl she appeared to be when she was with him, and I didn't know why. I really didn't see why he was so enamoured with her.

As though sensing I was there, her head lifted, and she looked straight at me. Her eyes narrowed and her back went straight. She stared me down, completely unimpressed. I should have been in Bailey's class watching and learning, but, not one to back down from a challenge, I angled my head and studied the girl who was in Bennett's arms moments ago. Did she know who I was to him? Had he been stupid enough to tell her? Maybe she was jealous. Or furious. I couldn't tell.

It was when she brushed the hair out of her face that I noticed her scars—they seemed to cover one side of her body—and I realised who she was. Bennett and I didn't really talk about a lot of personal things. Our relationship, if you could call it that, was…had been more physical than anything. But when he did open up and talk, he always spoke of this girl. His friend who had lost her entire family in a house fire and had almost died herself. She was that girl.

My heart pounded in my chest, and my palms were sweating. The heavy feeling in my stomach intensified as we stared at each other. She was more than a friend to him, I just knew it. There was something in the way he spoke of her that made me think there was more to their relationship than friendship. But it was easy to brush it aside and ignore it when I didn't know who she was. When she was no one to me. Now, though, I had to see her every day. She'd be in my class with him, and there was nothing I could do about it.

Bennett and I were over the moment I walked into Bailey's classroom and I saw him sitting there. I couldn't have an affair with a student. It would destroy both our lives, our reputations, everything. But it didn't mean I wanted to see him with anyone else. With her. The girl with the scars. The girl who was more important to him than I was.

I swallowed the lump in my throat, turned, and walked away without another glance.

Bailey was furious when I walked into class late. Nothing new there.

"Sorry, I got lost." My excuse was weak, and she knew it was a lie. We'd spent five years at this school. I knew my way around just as much as anybody else.

The look she gave me caused shivers to run up my spine. I smiled. The girl finally grew a backbone. I guessed Ryder was right for her after all.

I sat in the corner of the room and tried concentrating on what Bailey was saying. I needed to pay attention if I wanted to pick up where she left off at the end of the week, but my mind was elsewhere. It wasn't until the two girls sitting at the table nearest to me started talking that I finally paid attention. To them, not Bailey. She bored me to tears with long-winded explanations. I'd never met anyone who got so excited over literature. Eyeroll. Groan. Whatever.

The two wannabe princesses at the back of the class had my full attention the moment Bennett's name was mentioned.

"He's so hot." Girly giggle.

He was more than hot. It was almost indecent. He was perfection.

"I mean, his arms." Insert dramatic sigh.

His arms were pretty fucking spectacular. Strong. Steady. Capable.

"Why her?" Scoff.

Her? Audrey?

"She's a freak. He just feels sorry for her." Hair flip.

"I'd die if he looked at me like that or put his arm around me."

Totally worth it.

"She's a slut. Have you seen the other guy who picks her up sometimes?" Raised eyebrows.

My ears perked up at that comment. Another guy?

"What, no?" Gasp.

Oh, my god. Why did I choose to come back to high school? They were so goddamn pathetic.

"She's totally playing two guys. Bennett and the guy with the cherry red truck."

"She must be great in bed. Why else would they want anything to do with her?"

"Yeah, I don't get it."

I sat back and straightened my shirt. Ran my hands over my pants. Tapped my fingers on my knees.

Two guys.

Was he stupid?

Did he know?

Of course, he did. He was screwing me and probably her at the same time. And neither of them cared. Why would they? They were young. They had their whole lives to figure this stuff out. It was all fun to them, like it had been to me once upon a time. But I grew up, something they had yet to do.

Pulling my focus back to Bailey and what she was doing with the rest of the class, I ignored the girls and tuned out their gossip. If there was one thing I knew, the gossip mill at this school was rampant.

After class ended, Bailey pulled me aside to talk.

"You need to pay more attention, or you're going to screw up everything all these kids have worked for," she said.

"Relax. I can handle it." I stretched my neck and rolled my shoulders, feeling uncomfortable after sitting in the corner of the room for so long, and glanced over my shoulder, out the door.

I wasn't an idiot. I studied. Got a degree and everything. Also, I could hand out revision sheets and notes without her holding my hand.

"Got somewhere to be?" Bailey asked as she packed away her files and folders on her desk.

"Yeah. Home. Is that all?" I really just wanted to get out of there, away from the students and Bailey harassing me. Away from Bennett and his little girlfriend. I wanted to go somewhere to clear my head.

"Yes."

I didn't wait a second longer. I turned and walked out the door without so much as a goodbye.

"But, Christina," Bailey called after me. I froze and winced, turning to look at her again. Why couldn't she just let me leave? "Make sure your head's on right tomorrow, or I'm going to speak to Sawyer."

I nodded once, still frozen to the spot, waiting for her to say something else. There was always something else.

"Okay. You may go," Bailey said as she picked up the duster and turned to clean the blackboard.

She dismissed me, like I was one of her students.

Me?

Whatever.

I was free, at least for the night.

I left Bailey to do whatever it was she needed to do and rushed down the hall, in a hurry to put as much distance between this school and me as possible. But I came to a screaming halt, almost losing my balance and slamming into Bennett and Audrey. They were at her locker together.

"Whoa, you okay there, Ms. Brown?" Bennett asked. His soft pink lips tipped up into a smirk, briefly flashing the dimple on his cheek as he reached out and steadied me. Butterflies took up residence in my belly like they often did when he touched me.

"I'm fine. Thank you." I glanced at Audrey, wondering if she knew about me. Deciding to act as natural as possible in case she was as clueless as I'd hoped, I continued. "Just need to watch where I'm going."

My eyes drifted to where Bennett's fingers were still on my shoulders, the heat from his fingertips caressing my upper arms. My heart thudded in my chest, and I swayed on my feet, wanting to lean into his touch. I cleared my throat and shook my head, and Bennett suddenly dropped his hands and stood back. Audrey pressed closer to his side and lowered her head, not wanting to make eye contact with me at all. Bennett's arm hung around her shoulder and held her close.

"Right, well, have a good night," I said and walked away before I did something stupid like question their relationship. I was their teacher, so it shouldn't have mattered to me at all. But it did.

He was in high school. I was his teacher, and yet I still wanted to feel his touch. Make him smile. Make him scream.

And it was so wrong.

Why? Why couldn't we have met in another three months when he'd well and truly graduated? Why did he have to be a student? And so damn good looking?

"Ms. Brown?" A deep voice called my name just as I reached the door.

So close to freedom.

I paused, one hand on the door handle, one knotted in a fist at my side, as I turned and smiled at John. "How did your first day go? Any problems?" He returned my smile and ushered me out the door, holding it open for me while his hand on my back guided me out.

"Great. No problems." I forced a smile. *Other than the fact I had one of your students naked in my bed this morning.*

"Glad to hear it. If you have any trouble, my door is always open." He kept his hand on my back and walked with me down the steps. I shifted uncomfortably under his touch, but he didn't seem to notice. If anything, he closed the distance between us further.

"I'm sure I'll manage," I said, increasing my speed to get away from him. He was friends with my father, and I wasn't sure whether this was normal behaviour for him. I'd only met him once or twice at the golf club and was too young to really remember him.

He followed, undeterred. "Some of the kids can be quite troublesome."

I stopped and turned to face him, intending on putting an end to the conversation and ridding myself of my god-awful chaperone, when Bennett caught my eye. I faltered. I opened my mouth but forgot what I was going to say. He clasped Audrey's hand in his, her bag over his shoulder, and led her to a car that was idling across the parking lot.

John followed my gaze. "Ah, yes. They're particularly troublesome, those two. Bennett more so than Audrey, so if he should give you any hassles at all, let me know, and I'll deal with him."

Bennett gave me a lot of things, but hassles weren't one of them.

John brushed a strand of hair from my shoulder

27

and let his hand linger in the same place Bennett's had been only minutes ago.

I frowned and tried to step back. He was too close. There was no warmth in his touch. In fact, it made my skin crawl. I peered over his shoulder again to see if anyone had noticed how close he was and saw Bennett watching me. His gaze was intense, and I could see the tension in his jaw from all the way across the parking lot. The car had left with Audrey in it, and he was alone.

"Listen, John." I smiled through clenched teeth, and grabbing his hand from my shoulder, I dropped it at his side and stepped back. "I appreciate the concern, but I think the students are going to be the least of my worries at this school. I'll tell my father you said hello, shall I?"

He practically jumped back at the mention of my father. Shaking his head and chuckling quietly, he composed himself and put some much-needed distance between us. "Yes. Please. Tell him we'll meet for a game one of these days. It's been a while." And then he left.

With one last glance at Bennett, I got in my car and took off before he or anyone else approached me.

CHAPTER FOUR

Bennett

It was dumb and risky, and I'd promised Audrey I wouldn't do it, but I followed Christina home. I wasn't really following, since I'd spent nearly every night in the past couple of weeks at her place, anyway, so I knew exactly where she lived.

But what threw me was she didn't go home. She turned left instead of right and went straight instead of curving back around, ending up on the cliff overlooking the cove.

"Go home, Bennett," she said when I climbed out of my car and came up behind her. She was perched on the safety rail.

"You going to jump?" I asked, leaning forward. It was a hell of a long way down.

She scoffed and looked out at the horizon.

"So, you're my teacher, huh?" I rested my elbows on the bar, close enough that my arm brushed hers. I wanted to touch her.

"Yeah. You failed to mention you were a

student." Her voice was bitter. She was pissed. Understandably. And so was I, dammit. She hadn't told me she was a teacher either. Though it probably wouldn't have deterred me unless I had known she was going to be *my* teacher. She wouldn't look at me, and if she leaned any farther away, she'd plummet to her death.

"Yeah." I nodded. "And you failed to mention you were working for my father."

I slid behind her, wrapped my arms around her waist, and pulled her off the safety rail, not letting go until she had both feet planted firmly on the ground and her back pressed into the bar. Even then, I locked her in place with my legs, my hands braced on the bar beside her.

"You didn't ask." She pushed on my chest to try to get me to move, give her space.

"Neither did you." I didn't budge. I leaned in closer, pressing my body against hers. Six hours, I hadn't been able to touch her, and my body was screaming for her.

She sucked in a breath, her eyes darkening, and she softened against me. Yes.

"Wait." She tensed, placing a hand on my chest. "Your father?"

"Principal Douche. Figured you would have worked that out by now."

"John's your father?" She stared at me, understanding flashing in her blue eyes.

"Clearly." Had we not exchanged surnames? Probably not.

"We have a few things we need to discuss, don't you think?" She tipped her head back and closed

30

her eyes.

I leaned down, brushing my nose along her neck, breathing her in. "Does this discussion include picking up where we left off this morning?"

Her eyes snapped open, and she used all her strength to push me back.

I chuckled and raised my hands in defence. "Or maybe you can see my father about that. I mean, at least it's not illegal with him. And you're exactly his type." He liked them young and blonde.

"You're an ass."

"Never said I wasn't." I shrugged, placing my hands in my pockets and walking over to my car. She and my father looked terribly close after school. Even Audrey noticed the way he leaned toward her as he spoke, his hand on her lower back. He was a creep.

"Maybe I will," she called after me. "Seems like he could handle me. He's man enough. Has lots of experience."

I clenched my hands into fists. She was saying it on purpose. Tormenting me. Still, if my father so much as looked at her the wrong way, he'd wish he'd sent me to my mother's to live.

I leaned against my car and looked at her. She'd moved closer and was now standing with her back against the passenger door of her car, arms folded across her chest, making her cleavage so much more visible.

She frowned at me and didn't say a word. I smirked and waited her out. I had all the time in the world. I avoided home and my dad like the plague. I'd rather be anywhere but there with him. We only fought or ignored each other, and he preferred to have his own space, which suited me fine. I didn't like to look at him. We continued to stare at each other, not saying a word.

She sighed and pushed off her car and walked toward me. "My father and yours are friends. That's how I got the job. I've only met John a couple of times, and you never came up in conversation."

Figured. Why would he talk about me? I was his biggest disappointment, his greatest inconvenience, and if it weren't for the fact my mother was even more selfish than he was, he wouldn't even be in my life. But he was the lesser of two evils.

Both my parents were career focused. They'd had a brief affair. Mum was young, wide-eyed, naïve, and dad's assistant who just wanted to work her way to the top of the corporate world—or more like screw her way to the top. But then she fell pregnant with me and got greedy, made too many demands of Dad. Demands he couldn't possibly fulfil with a wife and daughter at home. It ended his marriage, tore apart his family—the one he cared about—and ruined his reputation. His wife left with their daughter, my half-sister, Willow, and he had to build a life from scratch all over again.

I lived with my mother for a while, until she found herself some bigshot CEO to support her, and then she lost interest in me. Her clothes, fancy jewellery, and flashy cars became more important, and she shipped me off to live with John. I'd been a thorn in his side ever since.

"No surprise there." I shrugged.

"What do you mean?" Christina tilted her head

and studied me.

We'd never had a meaningful conversation, other than how tight to make the handcuffs, and I wasn't about to start with my father as the topic.

"He doesn't exactly scream 'father figure,' does he? I mean, he was laying the moves on you after school."

"He what?"

"Don't be daft, Christina. You're telling me you didn't notice the way he stood too close, or let his hand linger on your body too long?" I scoffed.

"You certainly noticed, didn't you?"

"From the other side of the parking lot. Yes." She was so close again, I could just reach out and pull her to me. "Did it make you feel special?"

"No. It made my skin crawl."

"Good." My lips curved into a small smile. I was glad she didn't enjoy his attention.

We were silent again, watching each other. She licked her lips, and her fingers twitched in front of her. She looked as though she was fighting the urge to reach for me as much as I was.

"This," she raised her hand after a few more moments and flicked it between us, "is over. You know that, right?"

I knew she was right. It had to end, but that didn't mean I had to like it. We were great together. She was made for me, my hands, my body, and given enough time, it could have become something more. I said I was an ass before, but that wasn't true. I liked her and could maybe come to care about her more, but I wasn't that much of a jerk to continue this affair and risk her job, her

33

reputation—hell, even her freedom. Or mine. If my father discovered our relationship, he'd kick me out without even blinking.

I pushed off the car and closed the distance between us. Her breath caught in her throat as she lowered her head and looked at the ground. My left hand rested on her hip, and my right grabbed her hair, pulling it tightly until she was staring me in the eyes. Her entire body pressed against mine. I leaned down, and my body hummed, wanting to kiss her one last time but knowing I shouldn't. I brushed my lips against her cheek and smiled when she melted against me, trying to turn her face so I'd kiss her.

"I know," I whispered against her ear, and then I released her, stepped back, and opened my car door. "I'll see you at school, Ms. Brown."

Looking in my rear-view mirror as I drove away, I watched Christina close her eyes and stomp her foot like a child. She didn't want this to end any more than I did.

It didn't have to end, though. Not entirely. We just had to put it on pause for a couple of months, until she was no longer my teacher.

Should be simple, right?

I could keep my distance, keep my hands and lips and other parts to myself for ten more weeks. It wasn't like I needed her, or my life depended on having her nails scratching down my back. Ten weeks was nothing. Audrey would make sure I stayed away and kept my focus on school work, and not my English teacher.

CHAPTER FIVE

Christina

My bed was cold and empty. Completely uninviting. Entirely different from what it had been earlier that morning when I didn't want to leave the warmth of Bennett's arms.

But he was a student.

My student.

And the principal's son.

Could it get any more complicated?

The purple silk scarf still hung from the headboard, and the unmade sheets depressed me. I grabbed a pillow and a blanket from the cupboard and made my way into the living room where I planned to eat my weight in popcorn and watch home renovation shows all night and not think about the boy with the blue eyes and muscles for days.

Jesus, he was just a boy.

My heart stuttered in my chest, and my stomach churned.

35

How old was he?

I'd never asked, apparently. Because Bennett didn't look like a high school student. He looked like a man in every way.

I hugged the pillow to my chest. What if he was only seventeen? The thought made me sick to my stomach. I could go to prison for that.

I grabbed my phone from the coffee table and almost knocked the bowl of popcorn over at the same time.

Christina: How old are you?

I waited, anxiously staring at the screen for his reply.

Bennett: Feeling guilty, huh?

He punctuated his text messages with perfect grammar. Why was that such a turn on? Oh, my god. I was turning into an English nerd. Like Bailey.

Christina: Just answer the question.

Bennett: I'm sure you can figure it out.

Christina: Bennett!

Bennett: Yes, Ms. Brown?

My stomach fluttered. There was something appealing about the way he said Ms. Brown, even in a text message. With that perfect punctuation. Dammit. No. It was all so wrong. But it felt so right. Why did he have to be a student?

Christina: Don't play games.

Bennett: I like our games, though.

I liked our games too. He was a great team player. Always went above and beyond. I went into the kitchen and poured a glass of wine, hoping to settle my nerves, and when I returned, there was another text.

Bennett: Let's play a game.

Christina: I'm not in the mood.

Bennett: I'm sure I can get you in the mood. ;-)

My lips twisted into a smirk, but I washed it away with my grape juice. I wouldn't fall for his charm. I couldn't let it happen. Bennett could be very persuasive, and it wouldn't take much to convince me to go back on my word. We were over, and all I wanted to know was his age, to ease the fear eating away at me.

Bennett: Twenty Questions.

Christina: You want to play Twenty Questions?

Bennett: Yes. You started it.

Christina: Then answer my question.

Bennett: That's not how this game works. You answer my questions, and then at the end, you'll have your answer.

Christina: Okay, fine. I'll bite.

I cringed the moment I sent that text, knowing what was coming next. He liked it when I bit his shoulder, collarbone, chest…

Bennett: So, what you're saying is you want me to come over?

My bed was cold and empty. He'd certainly warm it up.

Christina: No. I'll play the game.

Bennett: And if I win, you'll bite, then?

Christina: Bennett!

Bennett: I feel like I'm about to get in trouble.

Christina: You are if you don't stop messing around.

Bennett: Will there be some sort of punishment if I don't?

I thought about the handcuffs in my bedside

drawer and smiled. They were fun. I thought he liked them a little too much.

Christina: I've had a sucky day. I'm tired and grumpy and just need an answer.

Bennett: Grumpy, because you miss me already?

Yes. Even though I shouldn't.

Christina: Grumpy because you're not taking this seriously.

Bennett: Okay, I'll be serious.

Christina: Forget it. I'm going to bed.

Bennett: Alone?

Of course, I was going alone. What did he think, that I jumped from bed to bed? Well, okay, maybe he could think that since we slept together the day we met, and I barely remembered his name. But, Jesus, was that what he really thought of me? Was I more invested in this, whatever we were, than he was?

Bennett: Shit. No, not like that.

Bennett: That came out wrong.

Christina: Fuck you, Bennett.

Bennett: Been there. Done that. Twenty times, to be precise.

He counted?

Bennett: You're going to bed without me? That was what I meant to say.

Bennett: Want some company?

His texts kept coming, and I had to stop myself from laughing, smiling as I pictured how worked up he must be, thinking he offended me. He hadn't. Not really. I was the first to admit I'd had many relationships in the past, no matter how long or short they lasted, one night or two years. But it didn't mean I liked having it pointed out so blatantly.

Bennett: I don't mind the biting.

Bennett: What are you thinking?

That was a loaded question. I was thinking I wanted him to come over and warm my bed. About how much trouble I could really get into, and whether it would be worth losing my job over.

Christina: Good night, Bennett.

Bennett: Wait!

Bennett: Twenty Questions. I promise you'll

40

have your answer at the end.

Christina: No more games?

Bennett: None. Scout's honour.

Christina: Fine.

Bennett: Question the first...

I waited, staring at my phone and watching for the little dots to appear, indicating he was typing a message. But nothing happened. No dots. No replies. For an hour, I sat with my phone in my hands waiting, and nothing.

Jerk.

I threw my phone on the table and punched my pillow into a better shape so I could get some sleep. Alone. In my living room. And not in my bed, because it was missing someone who should never have been there in the first place.

But it was useless. I wouldn't be able to sleep. Not when my body craved Bennett. Had I really got so used to having him around that I couldn't sleep without him? The thought was ridiculous. I didn't need a man. Hell, he wasn't even a man.

Boy.

He was just a boy.

I'd never cared so much before about not having someone there. My last boyfriend and I broke up, and I went on like nothing had happened, like I hadn't even had a boyfriend. Flings had ended, and I'd always adapted to being single. So, why was

Bennett getting under my skin?

Grrr.

He frustrated me more than anything.

My phone buzzed on the coffee table with a text. And then it buzzed again. And again. I contemplated ignoring it, but maybe it was important. And if it was important, I should at least check.

I had almost convinced myself that I was only checking whether the text was important and not that it was from Bennett. But really, I was hoping it was him and thinking maybe if we texted longer, I might actually fall asleep.

Bennett: Sorry, had a phone call.

Phone call for over an hour. Who was so important that he could talk for an hour? I wanted to ask, but we were done. It wasn't my business. Unless it was another girl. Audrey. Was he talking to Audrey about me? About other things? What did they have in common?

Shaking my head clear, I read his next text, hoping for an explanation.

Bennett: So…

Bennett: What are you wearing?

Christina: My pyjamas. It's late. I was asleep.

I wasn't, but he needn't know that. He left me waiting, and I was sick of his games.

Christina: Who were you talking to?

Crap. I shouldn't have asked that. It really was none of my business. But the idea that he had friends, someone else to share his time with, unsettled me. I had no one. No friends—that was my own doing, I knew that. Only Bennett. And I couldn't even have him anymore. I was destined to be alone. Perhaps it was karma for all the shit I caused when I was younger.

Christina: Never mind. It has nothing to do with me.

Bennett: Are you jealous, Ms. Brown?

Christina: No. Not at all.

Bennett: Sure. Where were we on this Twenty Questions game?

Christina: You got side-tracked and never asked a question.

Bennett: I did, and you answered. Not what I was hoping for, though.

Christina: What?

Bennett: I asked what you are wearing. Nineteen more to go.

Christina: Well…

I waited for his next question.

Bennett: Ms. Brown, it's a school night, and I really should get some sleep. Don't want to be late for my favourite class.

Christina: What class is that?

Bennett: Well, see, it used to be gym because I have great stamina and a lot of energy to exert.

Yes, I had firsthand knowledge of just how much energy he had.

Bennett: But now it's English.

I smiled like a schoolgirl.

Christina: Any reason why?

Oh, my god, I was flirting with a student. I knew better. I should stop, but he made me want to throw caution to the wind and invite him over.

Bennett: Smokin' hot new teacher.

I typed a response and deleted it, then typed another and cleared it. All the things I wanted to say and all the things I wanted to do, I couldn't. Instead, I wrote the only thing I should.

Christina: The last two weeks never happened. We do not know each other. Good night,

Bennett.

CHAPTER SIX

Bennett

Brody was rushing out the door when I pulled up at the Kellerman house the next morning and handed him a coffee. He took it from me and stared at it like I had poisoned it. His eyebrows pinched together, and his eyes narrowed as he focused on the paper cup.

"What's this?"

"A puppy. What does it look like? It's a coffee."

"Why?" He lifted it to his nose and sniffed, and I wanted to smack him in the face. He had that effect on me a lot. I liked to call it left over jealousy.

I snatched the coffee from his hands and placed it back in the tray I was holding. "If you don't want it, I'll give it to someone else."

"I didn't say that. I just…" He rubbed a hand over his face. "Why are you bringing me coffee?"

"Am I not allowed to?" Jesus, this guy. I tried to do something nice, and I got questioned about it. To be honest, though, I didn't buy him a coffee. They

46

screwed up my order and gave it to me for free.

He rolled his eyes and sighed. "You're impossible."

"Take the damn coffee." I shoved it back in his hand. "You look like shit."

He did. He looked exhausted. Maybe work was busy.

"Ah, thanks." He nodded once, looked over his shoulder at the front door, and said, "She's waiting."

"I know." I smirked and pointed to the front window where the curtain was pulled back slightly, and Audrey's face was pressed to the glass. Brody laughed and waved goodbye.

I walked into the house, and Audrey pounced on me. "Is that for me?" Her eyes lit up at the sight of the two smoothies I was holding.

"No. It's for our new English teacher. You know, to say welcome. Since the way I really want to welcome her is frowned upon in pretty much every bloody state in every country in the western world."

She wasn't impressed with that answer, if her punching me in the shoulder was anything to go by. I rubbed the spot she hit, pretending it hurt, and handed her the smoothie. She knew it was for her. I brought her one every day because I knew she rarely ate breakfast.

"There will be no welcoming the new teacher, in any way, shape, or form, Bennett Sawyer." She scowled but quickly smiled after taking a sip of her drink. "Cake batter?"

"Of course." It was really chocolate banana, but

the smoothie place I went to had a way of making things taste different from what they really were. Which, I had to admit, was great because some smoothies were revolting. "Ready to go?"

"Yep, let me just grab my bag." She walked off down the hall to her room and returned a minute later swamped in her hoodie with her bag in her hand.

"One of these days I'm going to get you out of the house without the jacket," I said and reached for her bag.

"No, you won't," she said, and then called loudly, "Bye, Leanne."

"Hi, Mrs. K. Bye, Mrs. K," I called out to Leanne, wherever she was.

Her head peered around the kitchen wall, and she waved. "Have a good day."

I opened the car door for Audrey and threw her bag in the back with mine. I was such a gentleman sometimes, it surprised me.

"So?" she said the moment I pulled out of the drive.

"So?" I tapped my fingers on the steering wheel in time with the music playing on the stereo.

"What did you do last night?"

"Talked to you on the phone." I glanced at her, catching her roll her eyes. Same thing we did every night. We had one of those friendships where we always had something to talk about, only last night the subject of Christina never came up, except for Audrey to tell me that I should stay far, far away from her.

"After that?"

I shrugged, not wanting to give her an answer because I knew she wouldn't like it.

"Bennett?"

"You probably don't want to know, bro."

"Does it involve She Who Must Not Be Named?"

"You're implying Christina is the same as Voldemort?"

She slurped on her smoothie before turning to stare at me. "If the cloak fits."

"The cloak?" I laughed.

"Or better yet, the witch's hat!"

"She can't be that bad. Maybe she's changed."

"Yeah, she'd want to have suffered amnesia or something, because there's no way someone that horrible could ever change, Bennett. She's not a nice person."

Maybe I saw something different in her than everyone else did. I chuckled to myself. I saw a lot more of her than anyone else had. In many different ways. I shifted uncomfortably in my seat.

"What's so funny?"

"Nothing," I said as I pulled the car into the school parking lot.

"You're thinking about her, aren't you?"

"Can you blame me? It's so much more exciting now it's not allowed."

"You're impossible."

"Funny, Brody said the same thing this morning." I turned the car off and sat there playing with the keys. We were early. "But seriously, I don't really know what happened back in high school, only bits and pieces, but it can't be that bad.

Everything is so much more dramatic when you're seventeen and trying to be popular."

"It was much worse than bad."

"So, fill me in."

"It's a long story, and we'll be late."

"I'm sure I can persuade the English teacher to let us get away with it."

Although, after last night's text messages, I was probably the last person Christina wanted to see. I would try to behave, but it just wasn't in my nature to do what I was supposed to do. I tended to rebel against everything my father said. I knew he wouldn't like this if he found out, and that made it so much more appealing.

"There will be no persuading," Audrey scolded.

I stared at her and waited. She shifted in her seat, slurped on her drink some more, and took a deep breath. "Okay, you asked for it."

I raised an eyebrow and smirked.

"Mind out of the gutter, Bennett. So, Chace and Ryder were best friends, and Chace dated Kenzie, Ryder's sister. Until he got her pregnant and demanded she terminate the baby, which she didn't because...Cole. But she felt she had no choice except to leave town because of the way Chace and his parents treated her. They tried to pay her off," Audrey said with disgust. "So, she ran off to her aunt's to have Cole and stayed away for a couple of years, too scared to come home because Chace is a giant dick face to everyone. Meanwhile, Chace moved on and began dating Bailey almost the instant Kenzie and Ryder left town."

"Wait." I covered her mouth with my hand

because that part didn't make sense, and she was going to keep rambling and waving her hands around everywhere if I didn't stop her.

"What?"

"One, Bailey wouldn't date Chace if she knew he'd done that to Kenzie. And two, if she did, then I can't see why Ryder would have been interested in someone who dated his sister's ex-b—"

"Dick face."

"Ex-dick face."

Audrey took a deep breath. "Because Kenzie didn't go to this school like everyone else. She went to school in Storm Cove, for whatever reason." I reached over and grabbed Audrey's hands to stop them flapping around before she gave me a black eye and held them on the console between us. It didn't even put a pause in her speech. "And Bailey didn't know much about Ryder at the time because, apparently, he was super quiet, and I guess, like, not popular," she whispered conspiratorially and giggled. "Let alone that he had a twin sister, until he returned to school after Kenzie was settled with her aunt, looking like the total badass he is now, just with fewer tattoos. And then everybody noticed Ryder Freaking Jones."

I quirked an eyebrow, and Audrey blushed. "Sorry, too much time with Indie and Bailey. Anyway, Bailey noticed him too. But she was dating Chace, and Ryder quickly got a bad reputation, which only made him hotter." She paused. "Don't tell Brody."

I barked out a laugh. "Secret's safe with me, cupcake."

51

"So, Ryder secretly pined for Bailey because he's a romantic and had been in love with her forever, hence why he hated Chace even more. Then Chace dumped Bailey in front of the whole school and hooked up with Christina a few weeks later. But it turned out..." she paused and looked at me, squeezing my hand tighter before speaking through clenched teeth, "Christina had been sleeping with Chace behind Bailey's back." Audrey sighed and shook her head. "I don't know how Bailey dealt with it. I can barely get myself out of your car in the morning to face the kids at this school, let alone having to see your ex-best friend and ex-boyfriend rubbing their relationship in your face every chance they got."

"It would suck. But you have me, and there's no way I'd ever hook up with Brody behind your back."

"You're an idiot," she said with a laugh.

"Besides, I'm into blondes now." Though after hearing the full story and realising why they all hated Christina so much, I should have probably focused my attention on brunettes. I shot a sideways glance at Audrey as she brushed her dark hair out of her face, her laugh fading into a silent scowl. No, not brunettes. That'd get me in as much trouble. Redheads. Fiery redheads would be the perfect distraction. Too bad I didn't know any.

The way Christina treated Bailey was a pretty fucking shitty thing for a best friend to do, so I understood why they all felt that way about her. But people changed all the time. Surely, she deserved a second chance. She was young and dumb, like everyone at this age.

I reached over into the back seat and grabbed our bags before we really were late for class. I couldn't afford any more detentions, otherwise I'd get suspended, and there was no way I could do that. I couldn't leave Audrey alone to fend off the wolves.

"I've noticed," she muttered and glanced out the window. Her face screwed up, and she squeezed her eyes shut. She struggled the most with walking into school in the morning or going into a room because she was still convinced all eyes were on her and that everyone was talking about her.

I hated it.

She had no reason to be embarrassed or feel ashamed. She was just as beautiful on the outside as she was on the inside, and if any of those wankers at school bothered to get to know her, they'd see it too.

I climbed out of the car, and like I did every morning, I rounded Audrey's side, pulled her out, and wrapped my arm around her shoulder. She fit perfectly beside me and snuggled against my ribs. Her confidence would grow slowly throughout the day as she relaxed a little, but the mornings were the worst. We walked inside and stopped by my locker to dump my stuff.

"Did you read the review sheets Bailey..." Audrey paused and looked around with wide eyes as she realised she referred to Bailey by her first name, which was frowned upon by Principal Douche, "I mean Ms. Mitchell sent home last night?"

I whistled a little tune and looked up at the

ceiling, avoiding her piercing gaze.

"Bennett?"

"Well, I was kind of preoccupied." I shrugged, grabbed her hand, and dragged her down the hall to her locker.

"With what?"

"Really, bro? You can't figure it out?"

"Don't tell me Ch—" she started, but I cut her off.

"Trying to get her to sext me." I grinned.

"What? You can't be that dumb." Her voice was high pitched as she turned by her locker and poked a finger in my chest. It was cute that she thought she intimidated me.

"Jacket?" I ignored her and held out my hand for her jacket. Hesitation flashed in her eyes, but also determination. She growled and pushed my hand away. "What, no help today?"

She just stared at me and stuck out her tongue.

"Real mature, Audrey."

"Coming from you?" She giggled as she looked from side to side down the hall before grasping my shirt and pulling me to stand directly in front of her. I stretched out my arms and placed them on lockers on either side of her. I was her shield. Her human dressing room—which wouldn't be so terrible if I at least got to peek down her shirt once in a while, but Brody would kill me.

She had this fear of removing her hoodie in public. I didn't get it. But she was confident that if she removed it, everyone would stop to watch "the freak" undress, and it gave her a panic attack just thinking about it. So, I stood guard in front while she discreetly stripped out of the oversized black hoodie I was sure came out of Brody's closet. Her fingers fumbled with the zip, and she dropped it four times.

"Dammit," she whispered.

"What's wrong?"

"You," she grumbled and lowered her head.

"Are you grinding your teeth?"

"No."

"I can hear it."

She fumbled again with her zip, and I reached down to stop her. "Relax," I said softly. "It's just us." I wrapped my hand around hers and pinched the zipper between her thumb and forefinger and pulled it slowly down until it opened and I could peel the jacket from her shoulders. "Want to tell me what that was about?"

"You."

I folded her jacket and put it in her locker. "You keep saying it's me, but you're not telling me why."

"Because you worry me, okay?"

"You don't have to worry about me. I'm great." I winked at her, waiting for a smile.

"We have ten weeks of school left, so stay away from her. Please." Audrey frowned up at me, and my chest tightened. She cared about me more than anyone ever had, and I owed it to her to try. I didn't want to do anything to jeopardise our friendship. She meant more to me than anyone else.

I nodded.

Her face lit up, and when she smiled, her right eye crinkled. She wrapped her arms around my waist and hugged herself to my chest before looking up at me. "You weren't serious about the sexting, were you?"

"Don't make me lie to you, bro." I rubbed my hand up and down her back. It started out as a way to calm her down or comfort her when she freaked, but it became a habit. I did it without even realising now. I was always touching her in some way, and she never complained, so I wasn't going to stop. I thought she liked it, the comfort I provided her, like a giant teddy bear.

"You really are that dumb," she groaned and smashed her head into my chest.

"Nope, just that horny," I said with as much seriousness as I could.

She let out a deep breath and pushed out of my arms. "I'm best friends with an idiot." Audrey crossed the hall to her homeroom, shaking her head in disbelief.

Picking up her bag and closing her locker, I called over to her, "But you love me anyway!"

"I question myself sometimes."

I crossed the hall and handed her bag over, and dropping a kiss on her head, I said, "I'll see you in English." And then I turned and walked straight in the direction Christina was standing with her arms folded and eyes narrowed.

CHAPTER SEVEN

Christina

He had the balls to smirk as he walked by. "Ms. Brown," he said and nodded once in greeting. His eyes never left mine. Meanwhile, I was plotting all the ways I could separate him from his little girlfriend. I didn't like the way he was with her. The way his eyes sparkled in amusement whenever she spoke. The way he always touched her. Held her hand. Draped an arm around her shoulder. The way he was putty in her hands.

I stormed down the hall to the bathroom just for something to do until class began. Inspecting myself in the mirror, I wondered whether I was too old. If things were different and I wasn't his teacher, would he have got bored of me and moved on to someone younger, like her? Did he want her? The way he looked at her and how he protected her made me think there was more than friendship going on between them.

It was all too confusing. Too complicated and

not worth it. He was just a guy. He helped pass the time, and that was it. There was nothing more to it. There couldn't be more to it. But…

The bathroom door opened, and I looked up. Audrey stood with her back to the wall and her eyes closed. She seemed to have no idea I was there as she rocked back and forth on the spot. Her fists clenched and unclenched, and she gasped for breath.

What the hell was wrong with her?

I took in her appearance. There was really nothing special about her. Compared to half the girls in this school, she dressed like a freaking nun, covered head to toe. I had to give her props for her boots, though. They were killer. Other than that, I couldn't see what had Bennett so obsessed with her.

The bell signalled the beginning of class, and Audrey still didn't move. A small part of me wanted to ask if she was okay. But a more significant part of me—the part that was jealous and insecure and wanted to keep Bennett handcuffed to my bed— didn't care and thought maybe, if I left, she might get in trouble, and it would put some distance between her and Bennett.

I opened my mouth to ask if she needed help but stopped. The more prominent, jealous part of me won out, and I walked straight past her and out into the hall without a second glance.

I headed for Bailey's classroom, to observe again like I was the damn student and not going to be taking over the class at the end of the week. It had briefly occurred to me that maybe she was forcing me to sit quietly in the corner of her class as a way of getting back at me for everything I did to her growing up.

I was a bitch. And Chace was so gorgeous, with his tanned skin, muscular arms and chest—nothing compared to Bennett, though—and his golden brown, sun-kissed hair. I practically melted at his feet every time he smiled, and I wasn't the only one. But I was the only one to act on it. I'd always been the type of girl to get what she wanted, regardless of the consequences, and Chace was no different. Only he was dating Bailey at the time. But back then, all I thought about was myself.

Would I do it again? That depended.

With Chace? No. Hell, no.

I was so stupid and naïve. I thought he loved me. I thought he wanted me more than Bailey, but the only person he loved was himself. He turned me into a horrible person, one I hardly recognised, and I hated who I became when we were together. I only wished I saw his hold on me earlier.

On the other hand, would I sleep with Bennett behind his girlfriend's back? Abso-freaking-lutely. But you couldn't hold that against me. He was perfection. I may feel a little more guilt about it than I did with Bailey and Chace, though something told me Bennett would never allow that to happen. If he had a girlfriend, that would be it. He'd commit to her, and no one else would stand a chance. Audrey was fortunate if she ever managed to get her head out of her ass and lock him down.

I slowed my approach when I spotted Bennett looking around the hall. Bailey walked over and smiled. "Bennett, what are you doing out here? You should be in class."

"Looking for Audrey." He turned again and scanned the hall.

"Maybe she stopped on her way somewhere. I'm sure she'll be here in a minute. Come inside."

Bennett gave her an incredulous look. "Where the hell could she have stopped on the eight steps from that room," he pointed across the hall, "to here?" He pointed at Bailey's class.

"I don't know. Maybe her locker."

"Not without me."

I hated the way he was so sure she wouldn't do anything without him. Like he expected she would wait for him, or they couldn't do anything alone. Co-dependency wasn't a good thing. It was bad. I knew from experience.

"She's just in the bathroom." I sighed as I stopped in front of them. Bailey narrowed her eyes at me, and Bennett sighed in relief. "She was leaning against the wall with her eyes closed, making fists with her hands."

"And you just left her in there?" Bennett growled, his posture changing instantly, and pushed past me, almost knocking me over.

"Unbelievable," Bailey muttered and followed Bennett. I wasn't sure whether she was talking about me or the way Bennett stormed off when he should have been in class, but I was willing to bet it was me.

I stood there staring at the bathroom door as it swung back on its hinges, wondering what I had missed. They had both looked at me as though I had kicked a puppy. And Bennett was currently in the female bathroom with a student. Unable to stay in the dark anymore, I walked to the bathroom again and pushed open the door.

Bailey stood to the side, while Bennett had Audrey cradled to his chest, rubbing her back and whispering in her ear. I felt like I was intruding, but I couldn't look away. I didn't know what was going on.

Bennett looked at Bailey and angled his head to the door. She nodded, placed a hand on his arm, brushed Audrey's hair, then walked out, not saying a word to me. His gaze landed on mine. It was cold, hard. And the tightness in his jaw told me he was pissed.

Whatever.

I shrugged and walked out.

I didn't know what was wrong. I didn't understand why she was hiding in the bathroom. I didn't care.

Not entirely true. Some part of me was curious. But mostly, I figured if she wasn't bleeding or crying on the floor, it was none of my business.

I made my way back to Bailey's classroom.

She was already in full teacher mode as she stood at the front and gave the students instructions and handed out more worksheets. I had to give it to her, she was prepared and organised. It would make my job easier once she left. It used to drive me crazy how much she liked her routine when we were growing up. Who'd have thought I'd come to appreciate it?

My phone buzzed in my bag, and I pulled it out discreetly, trying not to be caught by Bailey, to see a text from Bennett.

Bennett: Question the second…How could you leave her alone?

That was his question. He must have been pissed.

Because I didn't care. She was fine. A little dramatic, maybe. She really knew how to work him to her advantage. I'd never seen anyone go running after another like that. That bitter, jealous part of me reared its ugly head and wondered if I caused a scene, would Bennett run after me to make sure I was okay. I doubted it, though. I didn't have what she had. We didn't have that connection, that bond they seemed to share. All we had was explosive chemistry in bed, but one look at Bennett, and you knew he could find that anywhere. I wasn't special.

Audrey was.

Christina: Because I didn't know anything was wrong.

Bennett: Bullshit.

Christina: It's true.

Bennett: I saw your face earlier.

Bennett: Are you jealous?

I dropped my phone back into my bag and ignored his text. I was utterly jealous, but I wouldn't give him the satisfaction of knowing that. Instead, I turned back to Bailey and paid attention to what was going on.

Bennett and Audrey returned about ten minutes later, with Audrey—surprise, surprise—nestled safely under Bennett's arm.

I rolled my eyes.

May have snorted.

And refused to meet his gaze. I didn't want to see the smug look on his face.

"Sorry Ms. M. We, ahh…got held up." Bennett lifted a shoulder and explained to Bailey why they were late like she didn't already know.

"That's okay. Take a seat." She smiled and observed Audrey.

The girls sitting in front of me began laughing behind their hands and whispering to each other.

"Yeah, I bet they got held up."

"I saw him go into the girls' bathroom."

I cleared my throat and raised an eyebrow at them.

They shut up.

It wasn't that I cared they were talking, I just didn't particularly want to listen to them spout rumours about Bennett.

My phone vibrated again, and my eyes immediately searched for Bennett. He lifted his chin a fraction, as though challenging me to look. I turned away and crossed my arms over my chest.

Bailey was talking about an essay, and I tuned out. I couldn't focus with him in my class. Against my will, my gaze travelled to Bennett again, this time to see Audrey leaning against him, forehead pressed into his shoulder while he stroked her hair.

I swallowed the lump in my throat and reluctantly pulled out my phone.

Bennett: How about now?

I shook my head. I wasn't playing his games. I was done.

CHAPTER EIGHT

Bennett

"Wanna get out of here?" I asked Audrey the moment English was over. I didn't want to hang around any longer. She was one step away from having a breakdown, and I didn't even know why.

It hurt walking into that bathroom and seeing her slumped against the wall with her head between her knees, trying to catch her breath. I hated seeing her that way. It had been a while since she'd had a full-blown panic attack, and she was still jittery.

"Please." She smiled and nodded.

I reached for her hand and picked up both our bags before dragging her out of Bailey's class, straight past Christina, without a word to anyone. I was sure Bailey knew we'd leave and would try to cover for us, but who knew about Christina. She was impossible to read sometimes.

Just when I thought she couldn't possibly be as bad as Audrey had made her out to be, she went and did something like that. She left Audrey alone in a bathroom when she was having a panic attack. She probably wouldn't have even mentioned it, had I not been looking for Audrey at the same time Christina left the bathroom.

We skirted around the students taking their time in the hall and darted out the front doors, not stopping to check whether anyone had seen us. I half expected to be stopped by my father. It was like he waited for me to screw up most days, always there when I didn't want him to be and never around when I needed him. But we made it to my car without an issue.

I helped Audrey in, dumped our bags in the back, and raced around to my side, eager to get the hell out of there.

"Where do you want to go?" I asked.

"Anywhere?"

"Hungry?" I asked as I pulled out of the parking lot.

"No."

"Liar."

We drove in silence, straight to the roadhouse on the outskirts of town. It belonged to Johnny and Julie, an older couple, but they retired and left it in the hands of their nephew Jeremy and niece Harper.

Jeremy was dating Ryder's sister Kenzie, and Harper just so happened to be dating Nate, Brody's cousin. Nate was a great guy. I liked him. He was kind of like Audrey's foster brother.

Nate's parents had taken Audrey in almost a year ago after the fire that killed her family and nearly killed her. He didn't live at the house, though. He had shared an apartment with Brody for a while, until Brody discovered Nate was banging his ex-girlfriend, Harper, behind his back, and Brody moved out and straight into the Kellermans' house. It was all a big deal and lots of drama, and they didn't speak for a long time until Brody got over it and realised he'd fallen in love with Audrey during all the time they spent together.

As much as I didn't like to admit it, they were perfect for each other. He and Nate saved her life in that fire, and now they had an unbreakable bond, and that was something she needed.

"The diner?" She screwed her nose up when I pulled into the parking lot.

"Best burgers in the state," I reminded her. They were pretty amazing. "It's quiet," I prompted after looking around and not seeing too many cars. Bailey's husband Ryder's car was parked around the side near the garage where he was talking to Jeremy. He helped Jeremy run the place when he wasn't busy running a bookstore in town. Who'd have thought studying business would actually pay off?

"Okay. But only if I can get a rainbow milkshake," Audrey replied, and I tried not to gag at the thought of the milkshake Johnny had made up for her one day. It was purple and blue and pink with edible silver sparkles and whipped cream, and sure, it looked pretty—pretty disgusting—but she loved it.

"Anything you want."

We got out of the car, and Audrey came over to my side immediately. I pulled her in the direction of Ryder and Jeremy, and she groaned, apparently not wanting to see anyone.

"Can't be rude, bro."

"Shouldn't you be at school?" Ryder asked as we approached.

"Student free day," I answered. I was quick-thinking sometimes.

Ryder crossed his arms and raised a pierced eyebrow. He sure as hell didn't look like a guy who had a business management degree. He was covered head to toe in tattoos and piercings. Every time I saw him, I could swear he had more.

"What?"

"Did you forget my wife is your English teacher?"

"You're married to Christina?" I feigned shock and gasped.

Jeremy chuckled and muttered, "You're a dead man." And that made Audrey giggle, so it was completely worth it.

Ryder didn't even acknowledge the comment, he just glared at me. If I'd been smaller, I probably would have pissed my pants from his look alone, but I was taller, broader, and better looking than he was, so I didn't.

He looked at Audrey. "You okay, love?"

Love. Every time he said "love," the girl's underwear combusted. I tried it once, and Audrey punched me. Seemed it didn't have the same effect coming from anyone but Ryder. I didn't get it.

Audrey let out a shaky breath. "Bad day."

"Hungry?" he asked.

"Starved." She rubbed her stomach, and my mouth dropped open.

"You've got to be kidding me!" I said.

"Come on, I'll fix you something," he offered before asking Jeremy and me, "You guys want something?"

"No," I grumbled. I asked her two minutes ago if she was hungry, and she said no. He calls her love once, and suddenly she's starving and walking off into the sunset with Ryder freaking Jones. Fine, it wasn't the sunset, it was a grease-filled diner full of burgers and booze. Heaven.

Girls.

They were so complicated.

Women, on the other hand…

Were just as freaking complicated and confusing. I'd never win.

"Dude?" Jeremy's voice broke me out of my thoughts.

"What?"

"Got a proposition for you."

"What's that?" I eyed Jeremy curiously.

He was similar to Ryder. He also had the tatts from neck to ankles, but not as many piercings, though. The attitude was almost as bad too. The only difference was he didn't make the girls swoon like Ryder. And I meant all of them, except for Kenzie, obviously, because she was Ryder's sister and dating Jeremy. But Bailey, Audrey, Indie, and Harper all melted in a puddle at Ryder's feet. Even Leanne, Nate and Indie's mum, couldn't help but get a little crazy in the eyes when Ryder was around.

"A job."

Crap. Jeremy was still speaking. "Huh?"

69

"I need a little extra help around here on the weekends. Inside is growing. The garage is growing. It's too much for Ryder and me, and Harper has her final exams coming up, so she needs to focus on those. What do you say?"

"Does it include burgers?"

"And booze after knockoff."

"Then you have yourself a deal." I reached out to shake his hand.

"Thanks, man. I appreciate it."

For an ex-con, he was pretty polite and well behaved. Seemed to have adjusted well to being on the outside and was making a good life for himself and Kenzie and her son Cole. I respected that. I had to admit, Audrey had a great group of people around her.

I left Jeremy to it and went in search of Audrey. She was sitting at the counter, head lowered, hair fanned out to cover her face, sipping on her milkshake Ryder must have made.

"Good?" I asked, taking the stool beside her as the waitress flicked her eyes between us, lips twisted.

Audrey's face was drained of colour, pasty white, different than her normal olive skin tone, and her hands were trembling so much she could barely hold her the straw in her drink. "Bro?"

She shook her head rapidly and squeezed her eyes shut. I had no idea what happened at school to cause her to freak out like this. Her arms were covered in goose bumps, and she was rocking back and forth ever so slightly. Maybe I should call Brody.

No, screw that.

She was my friend. I could do this.

My eyes widened.

Her arms were covered in goose bumps.

Her arms were bare.

Her hair was in her face. Not her hood.

Her skin on full display.

Shit.

"I'll be right back." I stood and kissed the top of her head before jogging out to my car and yanking open the back door.

I searched through her backpack and my bag and came up empty. I checked the floor, the seat, everywhere. Nothing.

We'd left her hoodie at school, balled up in her locker. No wonder she was sitting inside, a complete mess. There were three customers I noticed in my rush to get out to the car, the waitress, Ryder, and I was sure there was someone else floating around the back. There always was.

I needed to get her out of there. Locking my car, I ran back inside to see Ryder whispering to Harper in the corner. She looked at Audrey, rolled her eyes, and held up her finger to indicate she'd be back in a minute, before darting up the stairs to her apartment above the diner.

I walked over to Audrey, stood behind her, and pressed my chest against her back. She leaned back into me, so I wrapped my arms around her. "I'm sorry. I didn't think. I just wanted to get you out of there." I looked around, trying to find something I could give her to wrap around herself in place of her hoodie, but there was nothing. It was me, or my shirt. That was all I had to offer. "Want my shirt?"

"Dude! Keep your clothes on," Ryder hissed and stepped behind the counter to grab me a bottle of water. "Harper's coming back." He walked into the kitchen.

I tightened my arms around Audrey protectively and used my body to shield her from the view of the other customers, the ones who weren't even paying her any attention or looking in her direction. Most people, honestly, usually looked straight past her. Their eyes may linger for a second—out of shock, I guessed—before they'd move on and not give her a second glance. This fear of people staring at her was entirely in her head. Most days she seemed to improve and was able to push the feeling aside, but for whatever reason, today she was struggling.

"Here." Harper's voice was soft as she stopped beside us and held out her hand. "It's Nate's."

I took the material from her, noticing it was a grey hoodie. It was huge, perfect for Audrey. "Thank you."

I placed the jacket around Audrey's shoulders, raised her trembling arms and pushed them into the sleeves, and smiled when she took a deep, shaky breath to calm herself down.

"Want to go for a walk?" Harper asked Audrey.

I opened my mouth to say something, to stop her, wanting to keep Audrey with me where I could look after her, but Harper smiled and nodded reassuringly. "Bennett, you can bring the food out when it's ready."

"Where?"

"Out the back. You'll see." She grabbed

Audrey's hand. "Come on, I'll show you my favourite spot."

They left, so I sat at the counter and contemplated calling Brody. He'd want to know his girlfriend had a panic attack. He'd also probably walk out of work and come straight down here to see her. I'd wait, get her to eat something, and then decide whether he needed to know now or later.

Ryder returned from the kitchen a few minutes later with a bag. "Wrapped it up for you. And made her a fresh shake." He handed over the food and paper cup full of sickly coloured milk.

"Any idea where they went?" I stuck my nose in the bag and inhaled the fried goodness. "Bacon burgers?"

"Breakfast." Ryder shrugged by way of answering. "The tower." He pointed through the kitchen to the back door.

"What tower?"

"You'll see."

I laughed. "What's with everyone around here not being able to give a straight answer?"

Ryder pinched his bottom lip and stared at me, still not saying a word. Then he clapped a hand on my shoulder and left. Figured. He wasn't much for talking.

I grabbed the food and Audrey's milkshake and snuck through the kitchen and out the back door, into the field behind the roadhouse.

There was an old car rusting on a patch of dirt, and dry, yellow grass as tall as my knees. Someone badly needed to get the ride-on out and cut it. A few patches of flowers grew. I didn't know what sort.

They were blue. Maybe purple. And trees lined the property border. I'd never noticed how big the property really was until right then.

I looked around, trying to locate Harper and Audrey anywhere, but they were completely out of sight, and then I remembered Ryder said something about a tower.

I squinted up at the water tower on the left side of the field. No way.

There was Audrey, perched at the top with Harper, and if my eyes weren't mistaken, she was laughing. It wasn't often that she smiled or laughed with other people because she was so self-conscious about her appearance, but when she did, it made my heart stutter. Shit, I sounded like a freaking girl.

I held the bag of food between my teeth and Audrey's milkshake carefully in the other hand and climbed the rickety old ladder to the top.

Pausing to catch my breath, I handed Audrey the food and drink and looked around. The view was incredible. Down in the far corner, I could just make out a stream, and I was sure if I walked around the other side of the tower, I'd be able to see all the way into town.

"This is your favourite place?" I asked Harper.

"Yep. I love it up here." She smiled. "Anyway, I better go."

"Don't leave on my account." I held up my hands to stop her.

"No, I have to study before I go to work tonight, anyway. I'll see you guys later." She stood and brushed off her pants before climbing down the ladder.

I sat next to Audrey and picked up her hand. "You okay?"

"Better."

"What happened?"

She shrugged in response. "I don't know. I can't explain that one."

She never had an attack come on for no reason, like this morning, and that was what scared me the most. Usually, she'd be able to pinpoint what sparked the anxiety and deal with it, but it was alarming when she couldn't figure it out.

I pulled out the two breakfast burgers Ryder had cooked. The dude really knew how to work a grill. Sunday night dinners at the Kellerman house tended to consist of Ryder's burgers, and he had an unlimited number of types he liked to make, with different toppings, sauces, cheeses, salads. They were to die for. "Anything said in homeroom?"

"No more than usual." She peeled back the wrapper and looked at the burger. Her lips twisted in disgust, and she folded it back up and put it down.

"I thought you were starving."

"Lost my appetite."

"Eat. You'll feel better. It's just your anxiety." I picked up her burger and handed it back to her. "We're not leaving here until you eat it all."

And we didn't.

We sat at the top of the water tower all day. Not speaking. Not eating. As much as I tried to convince her, my attempts were futile. We didn't do anything until Brody showed up.

"Thanks, man." He clapped me on the back

when he reached the top of the tower. "I'll take it from here."

I pressed a kiss to Audrey's head. "I'll talk to you later." And then I climbed down the ladder and left them alone.

Maybe Brody could figure out what caused her to freak out the way she did. That way, I'd be able to help her avoid another similar situation in the future.

I stopped by the workshop on my way out and spoke to Jeremy about shifts and when he wanted me to start.

"Soon as you can, man. With the kid on the way, Ryder will be even more tied up, and I need all the help I can get."

I promised I'd start the next day after school. Anything to get away from my father for longer periods of time.

I left the roadhouse and drove around for a while, not wanting to go home, and not having anywhere else to go. I should have asked Jeremy if I could start work then instead of tomorrow.

Stopping my car at the top of the cliff, I climbed out and leaned against my door. Toying with my phone, I contemplated texting Christina, even though I knew I shouldn't. It was wrong. We were over. And I was still pissed at her for leaving Audrey a mess in the bathroom. But I still wanted to see her, even after that stunt this morning.

She was supposed to be a teacher. Any normal teacher would have cared enough to make sure Audrey was okay. The only thing I could think of that would cause Christina to ignore Audrey like that was jealousy. She had to be jealous of my friendship with Audrey…or she really was as big of a bitch as everyone made her out to be.

CHAPTER NINE

Christina

Bennett had ignored me all week, which both pleased me and pissed me off. I didn't like being ignored. I wanted his attention, but I knew it was wrong, and I knew I needed to move on and forget I'd ever met him.

It was hard, though, because he flaunted Audrey in front of me, and I got the impression she didn't like me very much. Perhaps because I left her to have a panic attack in the bathroom alone, but she wasn't my problem. I'd managed to find out from Bailey that they were just friends, and Audrey had a boyfriend, but it still didn't quell the jealousy. I couldn't wait for the week to be over so I could hide away in my apartment and not have to see his handsome face, or her.

It was Thursday night, and I'd somehow been roped into the going out for dinner and drinks to farewell Bailey. I didn't know what idiot organised goodbye drinks for a pregnant woman, but the last thing I wanted to do socialise with a bunch of pathetic forty-year-olds who probably still lived at home with their mothers...with the exception of Carter, the PE teacher.

I watched him from across the table as everyone waited for Bailey to arrive. For someone who lived by a schedule, I was amazed she hadn't shown up yet.

Carter was handsome in a traditional way with his square jaw, deep-set brown eyes, and dark hair that was styled to perfection. He knew he looked good, but he didn't seem to abuse it or use it to his advantage. He was laidback and easy to get along with. He also appeared to have the attention of everyone in the bar, myself included. The thought had crossed my mind that maybe he'd be an excellent way to rid myself of Bennett.

I shouldn't be pining after a high school student.

I should be throwing myself at men like Carter.

"Here she is!" Carter smiled and climbed out of the both to greet Bailey with too much enthusiasm. He gave her a hug, kissed her cheek, and rubbed her stomach.

Ryder's nostrils flared, his hands were fisted at his side, and even from where I was sitting, I could see the tick in his jaw and the vein pop in his neck as Carter touched his wife and child. Some things apparently never changed.

Carter introduced himself and shook Ryder's hand, who looked at it in disgust at first before schooling his features and giving him an easy smile. Ryder dragged his gaze around the group until it landed on me.

If looks could kill.

His eyes narrowed, and his jaw twitched again. He took a step forward. Bailey, apparently sensing he was about to approach me or make a scene, placed a hand on his arm and stopped him with a barely noticeable shake of her head. He whispered to her, and she smiled at him before he walked over to the bar. He ordered drinks and chatted with the bartender, greeting him with a fist bump like they were good friends, before he returned with soda water for Bailey and a beer for himself.

I twisted uncomfortably in my seat. I felt out of place. I knew no one, not really. I'd only been at the school for four days. I didn't know what I was thinking when I'd agreed to come out. I should have stayed home with my wine and popcorn and watched home reno shows.

I pulled my phone out and pretended to be texting, just to give myself something to focus on, when it buzzed in my hand, and Bennett's name appeared in a text window.

Damn.

I really should delete his number, but that would seem so final.

Why did I finally have to meet a guy I liked, who was normal, and he turned out to be my student?

I could change schools.

I brushed that thought aside almost as soon as it occurred. No guy was worth ruining my career over, not even a six foot four, blond Adonis with a body that would rival any superhero.

I opened the message.

Bennett: Question the third. Do you ever just lay down and look at the stars?

What? I frowned at my phone. What was he talking about? If it weren't for the fact it was a school night, I'd have thought he'd been drinking. Maybe something was wrong.

Christina: No. Are you okay?

Bennett: I'm the one asking questions, remember?

Christina: You haven't said a word to me for days. Not since that episode with your girlfriend.

Bennett: She's not my girlfriend. It wasn't an episode. And you were a bitch. Just admit you're jealous of Audrey, and I'll move on.

Christina: I'm so not jealous. Why would I be? I've moved on.

Bennett: That quick, huh? Guess you haven't changed since high school.

I swallowed the lump in my throat. High school. He knew what happened in high school. But how?

Christina: Don't know what you're talking about.

81

Bennett: You're a sucky liar. I know about Bailey and your ex-boyfriend. I know everything.

If it was at all possible to feel the colour drain from your face, I did at that moment. I paled, and my stomach knotted. How could he know such a thing? His dad? Maybe, if my father opened his big mouth. But I doubted it.

Christina: How do you know about that?

I stared at my phone. He was playing with me. Again. I finished my drink and walked over to the bar for another one.

"Whoa, you might want to slow down, there," Carter said when I gulped down the fresh glass of whiskey.

"Bad day." It was a poor excuse, and it was more like a bad week. Month. Hell, a bad life. "I'll be back." I forced a smile and straightened. "Just need some air."

"I'll keep your seat warm." Carter smiled, and for a moment, I thought about asking him to dance, but I didn't want to lead him on. I knew what I said to Bennett was a total lie. I hadn't moved on. Not even close. I was just trying to keep my distance.

I grabbed my drink that the bartender placed down with a scowl, and before I could wonder what his problem was, I walked out the side door and around the back of the bar.

There was an old park bench under a single light, so I sat there and tilted my head back to look at the stars. I'd never really done it before, and Bennett had me curious. It was a clear night, and the Milky Way was visible. It was beautiful.

I was pulled from my thoughts by my phone buzzing again.

Bennett: That's for me to know. So, you've moved on, huh?

Christina: Yep. On a date right now, actually.

The lie came easily. Too easily, and that wasn't a good thing.

Bennett: And you're texting me? Must be boring.

Shit. I walked into that one.

Christina: He's on a call.

Bennett: In the middle of a date? Douchebag.

Christina: It's for work. He's a doctor.

Bennett: Question the fourth. Can you see Orion?

Christina: What?

Bennett: In the sky.

Christina: I'm on a date, in a nice restaurant.

Bennett: Yeah, and I'm totally not watching you from the top of the water tower.

Water tower. What was he talking about? I looked around and squinted, and sure enough, in the distance, I could make out a water tower in the field. A soft glow flashed, probably from his phone.

Christina: What are you doing there?

Bennett: Uh uh uh. I ask the questions. Question the fifth. What are you doing at the roadhouse on a school night?

He was asking what I was doing on a school night. Why was he creeping around the back of the bar?

Christina: Date.

Bennett: *scoffs* He's a keeper.

Christina: What's the supposed to mean? Are you jealous?

Bennett: Not at all. Just wondering what kind of loser brings a date to the roadhouse.

Christina: And where would you take a date?

For a moment, I let myself imagine what a date with Bennett Sawyer would be like. A real date, not a drink in sleazy bar. A date where he picked me up from my house and took me to a classy restaurant, not grabbing me and pushing me against the wall. Then maybe a walk along the beach in the moonlight or stargazing in a field like this one instead of sneaking into my house quietly in the middle of the night.

Bennett: Not a fucking roadhouse.

I climbed off the bench and moved in the direction of the water tower to speak to him when the back door opened, and Carter appeared on the back step.

Bennett: Who the hell is that?

Christina: My date.

I wasn't sure if he could see me very well from up there on the tower, but I smirked and put my phone away.

Maybe for just a second, he'd feel the jealous rage I'd been feeling all week.

"Just thought I'd check on you. You should come inside. It's not safe out here alone," Carter said as he approached.

I smiled and ignored the buzzing of my phone in my pocket as I followed Carter back inside. I could feel Bennett's eyes on me the entire way.

Back inside, Bailey and Ryder were at the bar talking to the bartender, who scowled at me again when I walked over to get a water.

"Christina, I didn't expect you to come," Bailey

said as she put herself between Ryder and me. Probably to stop him from saying something. I knew how he felt about me and was sure if it was okay for a man to hit a woman, he'd have probably knocked me out a few times over the years.

I didn't hold it against him. I just wished we could all move on. I was trying to be a better person and didn't want the past to haunt me.

"Don't think you're special. I'm only here because I have to work with these people for now. Had to make a good impression." I was such a bitch. It was like I couldn't turn it off, even though I tried hard to. I guessed because I knew how they felt about me and that nothing I could say or do would ever make things right between us, I figured there was no point in trying.

"Right, well, enjoy your night, then." Bailey rolled her eyes and turned back to Ryder, who was pointedly ignoring me.

Sally, the school's receptionist, came over and began talking to Bailey about the baby and her plans for after she finished tomorrow, to which Bailey replied she was resting and taking it easy and trying to get as much sleep as possible before the little one's arrival. That conversation prompted every other female staff member to pounce and start gushing over Bailey and the baby she hadn't even had.

It was my cue to make myself scarce, and apparently Ryder's too. The bartender gave him a beer, and he moved away from the group of women surrounding Bailey. He headed straight for me.

"Christina."

"Ryder."

"How are you?" He practically choked on the words, screwed his face up as though the simple question tasted bad in his mouth. I stared at him, surprised he'd even ask how I was. It wasn't like he'd care.

I sipped my water and eyed him warily. I didn't trust him, and he certainly didn't trust me. "Great, actually."

"Are you living in town?"

"Storm Cove." I took a breath and continued. "Why are you talking to me? I'd have thought you'd come over here and threaten me to stay away from Bailey or something."

He chuckled, those famous dimples appearing on his cheeks, and he suddenly reminded me of the young man he used to be, with the boyish good looks and bad attitude. I guessed he hadn't changed much over the years. "Oh, there's a threat coming, don't you worry."

I gulped and shifted my feet nervously as he stepped closer. Years ago, he wouldn't have intimidated me at all. Or at least I wouldn't have let myself believe I was intimidated. Now, though, it was a different story. I'd seen firsthand how far he'd go to protect Bailey.

"But for some unknown fucking reason, Bailey begged me to give you a chance."

I raised my eyebrows and opened my mouth to speak, but no words would come out. Bailey asked him to give a me chance. Why would she do that?

"Yeah, my thoughts exactly," he said, as though he knew what I was thinking. "Damn pregnancy hormones make the woman crazy and irrational. And in the interest of keeping my balls firmly attached to my body, I'm going to humour her and be nice to you." He leaned in and brought his mouth close to my ear. "You mess with her again, or anyone else I care about, I will make your life. A. Living. Hell. I don't like you. I don't trust you. And I don't want you anywhere near my family or friends. So, stay away, and we'll get along peachy." He pulled back and stared at me with narrowed eyes, arms folded across his chest. "Understood?"

I nodded.

"Great." He clapped a hand on my shoulder and grinned. "Have a lovely night."

He walked off and left me standing in the middle of the dancefloor. My knees were trembling, and I could barely stand upright. He meant every word he said. I knew it. He was fiercely protective of Bailey and the people he loved, and I knew from experience he'd lay down his life or freedom for them.

He was the one person I maybe wanted to make amends with. Somehow.

"Want to dance?" Carter appeared out of nowhere.

"Umm…" I looked around, and no one was dancing. "I should get going."

"It's early. Come on. Let's liven this party up." He took my hand and pulled me to him.

Bennett was creeping around outside. Ryder was glaring daggers at me. Carter was right there in front of me. Free. Willing.

"What the hell?"

CHAPTER TEN

Bennett

Her date was not a doctor. Did she really think I didn't recognise our PE teacher, even from this distance? I laughed as I sent her the message calling her a liar. She ignored it, naturally, trying to make me jealous like I was sure she was jealous of Audrey. She said she didn't want to play any more games, yet she seemed to be playing them more than I was.

"I've never seen the roadhouse so busy!" Audrey huffed as she pulled herself onto the top of the water tower. "There are cars everywhere out there."

"Took you long enough," I said when she came to sit beside me. "I was about to leave."

"Sorry, we, ahh…got held up."

"I bet you did." I elbowed her gently in the side and made her laugh.

"Shut up." She ducked her head. "What made you decide to come here?"

"Well, after the other day when we were here, I

thought it would be a pretty cool place to stargaze, and who better to stare at the stars with than my bro."

I really just wanted time alone with her, away from the watchful eyes of Brody and the Kellermans, to make sure she was okay after her panic attack the other day. We'd not had much time together, since Brody had insisted on taking her to school and picking her up every day because he was worried. Like I couldn't handle it. But he was working tonight and dropped her here to hang out with me.

"Stargazing?"

"Yep." I lay down on my back and rested my head on the pillows I brought with me.

"You have a pillow?"

"I have two, if you want one?" I handed her a pillow and moved over, giving her room to lie down as well.

"You have pillows?"

"Yeah, for work."

"Work?"

"Uh-huh, so I can sleep out the back when I get tired. Or come up here on my break." What Jeremy didn't know wouldn't hurt him.

"How do you like the garage?"

"So far so good."

She shuffled around and tried to get comfortable. "Don't suppose you brought a mattress too?"

"Quit complaining."

"What are we looking at?" she whispered.

"The stars," I whispered back.

"There are millions of them. Wow. It's so

pretty."

"Why are you whispering?"

"I don't know." She laughed softly.

We stayed there, silently looking at the stars, only occasionally speaking when we found a constellation, or what we thought looked like something.

"Hey, I see a unicorn," Audrey exclaimed and pointed to a mass of stars that looked like, well, stars.

"You see unicorns everywhere."

"Because they're magical and give me hope. Nothing wrong with that."

"No, there's not. How are you coping after the other day?"

"Better. I'm sorry I freaked out and made you worry."

"That's what bros do." I shrugged.

She did freak me out, but once we realised the cause of her panic attack, it made it easier to fix. Sort of. I just had to keep my distance from Christina, which shouldn't have been too hard. Audrey meant more to me than anyone else, so I'd do whatever it took to make her happy.

Pathetic, really.

She wasn't my girlfriend. She didn't love me that way, but I still wanted to make her happy. And if that meant Christina had to be shoved out of the picture, I'd do it because I didn't want to be the cause of her breakdowns.

Audrey had been so worried about my relationship with Christina and the effect it would have on me if anyone were to find out. Combine that with the fact that Christina was probably the only person as despised as Chace by everyone we knew, and she couldn't cope.

"I still shouldn't have panicked like that."

"It just means you care." I poked her in the ribs, teasing. "You love me."

"Not if you're gonna get a big head about it." She sighed. "I just don't want you to get hurt."

"I'm a big boy. I won't get hurt."

"Still, I worry."

I wrapped my arm around her, and she rested her head on my chest. "Let me do the worrying. You just keep looking for unicorns, okay?"

"Okay."

Music filled the night air, and we rolled over to look at the back of the roadhouse. Light spilt out through the open door, and laughter echoed through the emptiness as two figures appeared, stumbling down the steps. They made their way over to the table where Christina had been earlier.

"They must be having a party inside," Audrey mused.

"Oh, yeah, it's Bailey's goodbye work drinks or something. Jeremy was telling me about it earlier when I was in there."

"Oh. Does that mean that…"

"Yes, and…" I squinted in the dark and looked at the two figures in the distance. A man leaned in and wrapped his arms around the petite blonde. "I think that's her down there."

"What?" Audrey screeched.

The laughter stopped, and Christina and Mr. Hamilton looked our way. We ducked out of sight.

They shouldn't have been able to see us all the way up here, anyway, though Christina knew precisely where I was, and I wondered whether that was her plan. Bring Mr. H. out here and put on a show to make me jealous. It wouldn't work. I didn't care.

"Is that Mr. Hamilton?"

"Yes."

Audrey turned to look at me. "I'm sorry, Bennett."

"Why? It doesn't bother me."

I couldn't even convince myself that was true, so I knew Audrey wouldn't believe me, but the fact was Christina and I were all sorts of wrong. We couldn't happen. It broke every rule there was, and a few laws too. If she had moved on, that was great. I needed to do the same. My problem was that the only other person I could imagine myself with was lying beside me and had a boyfriend.

And having feelings for your best friend never ended well. That was why Christina had been the perfect distraction. She helped me forget those feelings, and I started to move on.

Now...

I was lost.

Maybe I should just pick a random girl from school and take her out, get my mind off the two women I absolutely couldn't have.

Urgh.

But the girls at school were horrible. Airheads. Bimbos who spent more time looking in the mirror than they did at their textbooks. That was why I adored Audrey. She was smart, funny, beautiful— even if she didn't believe it—and fun to be around.

We clicked right away. Shame about Brody, but that was life.

"Want to get out of here? Go watch a movie?" Audrey offered.

"Sure."

I grabbed our pillows and climbed down the creaky old ladder first.

"Catch me if I fall?" Audrey asked, her eyes wide as she stared down at the ground.

"Why did you even climb up if you're scared?"

"Because you told me to meet you up there," she said with a shrug, as if doing whatever I said was the most natural thing in the world.

"I've got you. Come on."

I was a gentleman. I'd catch her if she fell, or at least fall with her and give her something to land on.

Once we made it to the bottom, I grabbed her hand and tugged her around the front to throw the pillows in my car, without even glancing in the direction of Christina and Mr. H. still pressed up against the picnic table.

"Want to go inside for a drink?" I turned to Audrey. "Something to eat?"

Her mouth twisted, and she shook her head.

"You sure? Bailey, Ryder, and Jeremy are inside. I feel rude, hanging around the back and not going in and at least saying hi."

"But she's there too." Audrey frowned and folded her arms across her chest. Her eyes squeezed closed, and I recognised the pained expression on her face. In a matter of moments, she'd start freaking out.

"Okay. Let's go, then. My place or yours?"

"Don't know why you insist on asking me that every time, Bennett. It's always my place."

"I'll surprise you one day." I laughed and opened the car for her, knowing full well that I'd never bring Audrey back to my house on the off chance she'd run into my father.

Closing the door after Audrey climbed in, I glanced back at the roadhouse one last time and noticed a figure, hiding in the shadows, peering around the corner at us.

Christina.

CHAPTER ELEVEN

Christina

It was Bailey's last day, and I was both excited and nervous. Excited because she'd finally be gone, and I could teach the class the way I wanted to. And nervous because she'd finally be gone, and I could teach the class the way I wanted to.

What if I screwed everything up?

I wasn't sure what sort of reaction I'd get from Bennett when we walked into class in the morning, and I really shouldn't have cared, but even after seeing Carter and me alone in the dark last night, I'd not heard a peep from him. I knew he saw me watching as he left with Audrey, and still he didn't say anything.

He could be jealous and bitter and sulking, not wanting to talk to me, which meant he cared and was struggling with ending things as much as I was.

Or he genuinely didn't care, which hurt. As much as I knew it was wrong, I wanted him to care. To fight for me. To wait for me until the end of the year when he was no longer a student.

It was selfish and stupid, but I couldn't help it.

The morning class progressed as usual. Audrey and Bennett huddled together in the back corner, and while I took every opportunity to watch him, he barely flicked his eyes in my direction. It was like I didn't exist. Even Audrey didn't pay me any attention.

The staff had organised a special morning tea to send Bailey on her way, and it made me wonder what the point of the bar last night was if they were doing the same thing again today without alcohol.

I had a meeting with Bailey at lunch, to which she was late, and her excuse was the baby was super active and kicking the hell out of her. She was in a bit of pain and moving much slower than usual.

Whatever. I just wanted it over with, so I could go and eat my lunch in peace and avoid Carter before he tried to get me to go home with him again. Dude didn't understand "no." Granted, I may have led him on the night before, but still...no. I wasn't interested.

The meeting was so Bailey could make sure I knew where each student was and what needed to be done before their final exams.

I rolled my eyes as she explained everything for the hundredth time, and then she did something I never expected. She apologised.

"Sorry. I guess I'm repeating myself. It's just that these kids have worked so hard, and I'd hate for them to fail so close to the end." She winced and rubbed her giant beach ball of a stomach, a small groan escaping her lips.

97

"It's fine. I've got this. You have two hours left until you're free. Relax. Put your feet up or something. You look awful."

She chuckled. "Thanks. I feel awful." She groaned again and rubbed her stomach. "This kid is crazy today. Ow!" She hunched over the desk and held her stomach before looking at me with wide, terrified eyes.

"What? Are you okay?"

She shook her head. "Christina, I need..." She gasped. "Ryder."

I raised an eyebrow. Like I could find Ryder even if I wanted to.

"I think the baby's coming." She stood, her legs struggling to hold her up.

"But you're not due yet."

"Two weeks, but it can happen anytime."

My hands trembled as she leaned on the desk for support, her other hand moving from her stomach to her back. I swallowed the lump in my throat. I didn't know what to do.

"I'll call an ambulance," I offered weakly, taking a step away. If the baby was coming, her water could break any moment, and I wanted to be nowhere near that mess.

"No. It'll take too long. I need to go now!"

I looked around the empty room and took a deep breath. *Man up, Christina.* "Let's go, then." There was no other option. It was either that, or she had the baby in the classroom.

"You? I need Ryder."

"He can meet us at the hospital."

She sucked in a deep breath through her nose and

let it out through her mouth with a nod. "Okay."

Taking a tentative step closer to her, I helped her stand and hoped like hell her water didn't break while I was next to her. With one arm around her waist, I led her out of the classroom into the empty hall. Everyone was outside or in the staff room enjoying their lunch, and I was stuck being a human walking stick for a pregnant woman who could drop that kid at any moment.

"Ahhh," she growled through gritted teeth and leaned against the lockers.

Once the contraction passed, we resumed our slow pace toward the front doors when Bennett and Audrey, of course, appeared in the hall ahead of us.

"Bailey!" Audrey rushed over. "What's wrong?"

"She's having a baby. What does it look like?" I snapped. I just wanted to get her to the car as fast as possible. "Bailey, where are your keys?"

"In my bag, in the staff room. There's no time to get them now. We have to take your..." She paused, leaned against the wall, and cried out again. "Car. Your car."

"Ahh, no. Sorry. I don't want that mess in my car. It's brand new." No way was she having a kid in my back seat. I'd never get that out of the leather.

"Move." Bennett's voice was deep and music to my ears. He shoved his keys in my hand and pushed me out of the way.

He lifted Bailey's arm and put it around his neck, and in one swift move, he hoisted her into his arms. "You get my car ready," he said to me and indicated with his head to the door. And you," he looked at Audrey, "call Ryder and tell him to meet us at the hospital. Let's go."

And with that, he walked down the hall carrying Bailey as though she weighed nothing.

We got to his car, and Audrey was frantically trying to reach Ryder. "He's not answering."

"Jeremy," Bailey gasped. "Try Jeremy."

Audrey nodded and jumped into Bennett's car, while I stood to the side and waited for Bennett to put Bailey down.

He looked at me and growled, "Get in."

I moved to get in reluctantly.

"Drive," he said, and then he opened the back door and manoeuvred himself into the back with Bailey.

"Jeremy isn't answering either," Audrey cried, her breath was coming hard and fast, and she looked like she was going to throw up.

I pulled Bennett's car out of the parking lot and headed toward the hospital.

Bailey cried out in pain, and Bennett whispered words of encouragement and reminded her to breathe. I watch him in the rear-view mirror, and my heart fluttered. He was such a good guy. I didn't deserve him. No wonder he wanted nothing to do with me.

"Try Romanov's," Bailey said, referencing the bookstore where she used to work.

"The bookstore?"

"Ryder runs it," Audrey answered as she put the phone to her ear again. Of course, he did. That was where they fell in love. "Thank god. Bailey's in labour. Meet us at the hospital. Me, Bennett, and…and Christina." She stumbled over my name when I assumed Ryder asked who Bailey was with. "Now."

She dropped the phone and turned in her seat to look at Bailey. "He's on his way."

Bailey nodded and groaned.

"Step on it," Bennett said. So, I did. I put my foot down and sped toward the hospital.

"Audrey, call my dad and tell him where we all are," Bennett said as I pulled his car into the emergency department and climbed out to open the door.

"It's okay, I'll go back. You two stay with Bailey. I'll finish her classes and bring your car back after school. If that's okay?" I couldn't hang around the hospital. I didn't want to be there when she had the baby or when everyone showed up. I didn't care.

"Whatever." Bennett rushed out again as Bailey tensed in his arms and cried out again. "You're going to leave some killer scratches on my back, Bailey. Too bad it's not more pleasurable for both of us," he joked.

And that bitter, jealous part of me bubbled to the surface once more. It should be me leaving scratches on his back.

Bailey laughed, and Audrey came around and smacked him. "Ryder will kick your ass. Come on."

Bennett gave me one last look and nodded before carrying Bailey in through the double doors.

CHAPTER TWELVE

Bennett

I carried Bailey through the doors and into the emergency department as Audrey rushed to the desk and explained what was happening.

"Bailey!" Ryder's voice echoed through the room as he burst through the front doors and rushed toward us. "You okay, love?" He leaned in and kissed her. I averted my gaze and looked at the ceiling, counting all the scuff marks up there, including a footprint. How a footprint ended up on the ceiling, I didn't know.

"What's going on?" Ryder looked at me.

"Don't know. She's been having contractions, I think. Pretty bad, couldn't move, so I carried her in here."

"Thanks, man."

Audrey came over. "They're getting her a wheelchair and taking her straight in."

A couple of seconds later, a nurse pushed a wheelchair over, and I placed Bailey in it carefully.

She winced but quickly covered it with a smile. "Thanks, Bennett."

I winked. "Anytime."

The nurse pushed Bailey away, and Ryder rushed along beside them. He was bouncing on the balls of his feet, hands running through his hair. He couldn't stop fidgeting, out of nerves or excitement, I wasn't sure.

"Can we come?" Audrey called out.

"You can come to the waiting room," the nurse answered. We followed them through the winding halls until the nurse pointed out the waiting area while taking Bailey and Ryder to wherever the hell people went to have kids.

Audrey and I sat in the hard plastic chairs. Who knew how long we'd have to wait?

Audrey pulled out her phone and laughed. "He's so excited."

"Ryder?"

"Yeah."

"Or scared."

"Check your messages." She waved her phone at me, so I pulled mine out of my pocket and laughed.

Ryder: I'm gonna be a fucking dad. Baby's coming!

"You think he sent that to everyone?"

"Absolutely." Audrey smiled.

"Which means that every—" I was cut off by the waiting room doors opening and Kenzie appearing, followed closely by Jeremy, "—one will be on their way."

"What's going on?" Kenzie asked.

"They've just taken them through. So, now we wait," Audrey answered.

Jeremy slouched in the chair beside me, while Kenzie paced the waiting room, running her hands through her hair, the same way her brother did, tugging on the ends and bouncing on the balls of her feet nervously. They were so much alike it was a little scary sometimes.

"How did you get here?"

"Christina." Audrey frowned. "She's such a bitch."

Kenzie stopped pacing and stared wide-eyed at Audrey. "What?"

"She drove Bennett's car here, while Bennett sat with Bailey, because she didn't want a mess in the back of her car if the baby came. I hate her." Audrey crossed her arms and pouted.

"She wasn't that bad. She didn't even have to drive here. She could have just called an ambulance and left Bailey alone. At least she tried to help," I said. Considering Bailey and Christina's history, I was surprised she even helped her out of the classroom, to be honest.

"You're *defending* her?" Audrey screeched. "After what she did last—" I shot her a warning glare, knowing she was going to bring up Mr. Hamilton and the bar last night, but she couldn't because we weren't alone. "Last time she lived here," she covered quickly.

"I'm not defending her. She was still a bitch, but she could have been worse. That's all."

And she was a bitch. I was beginning to see that

104

side of her. She didn't do things unless they suited her or were to her advantage. I'd paid close attention to her all week when she wasn't aware, and if things didn't benefit her, she had no interest in them. So, not wanting Bailey to birth a baby in the back seat of a ninety-thousand-trust-fund-dollar car wasn't that much of a surprise to me. But I had to believe a part of her was still the girl Bailey once called a friend. The girl who cared. Otherwise, she would have left Bailey high and dry to fend for herself the moment she realised the baby was coming.

"I still can't believe she's back." Kenzie resumed her pacing. "I don't trust her."

"I don't think anyone does."

"Anyone does what?" Indie asked, walking into the room with Linc. She looked at Audrey. "I called Mum and told her you won't be home until late and that Bailey was having the baby."

"Thanks. I forgot about Leanne." Audrey smiled.

Indie paced the room with Kenzie while Linc leaned against the wall. "So, did we all get the same text?"

I nodded, and Jeremy laughed. For a person who quietly observed everything that was going on around him and didn't show a lot of emotion, Ryder certainly flipped a switch when it came to Bailey and his unborn baby.

We sat quietly for a while until Harper arrived with her Uncle Johnny and Aunt Julie, the ones who owned the roadhouse.

"Where's Nate?" Audrey asked.

"He and Brody are working the same shift. They

should be here soon." She looked at her watch and shrugged. While Brody was a paramedic and worked crazy hours, Nate was a fireman and worked different shifts as well. Harper looked at Linc. "You couldn't get dressed?"

Linc frowned and looked down at his clothes. "I have shorts and shoes on." He shrugged. "I'd just put my board in the water when Ace came running to tell me we had to go. She didn't give me the chance to get changed," he said to explain why he was in boardshorts and sandals with no shirt. "The waves were good too." He crossed his arms and narrowed his eyes at Indie.

"Quit pouting," Indie teased her fiancé. "We live on the beach, and there will be more waves. But only one baby Jones."

"Well..." Kenzie interrupted. "What's Cole?"

"Oh, he's going to be a Donovan," Indie laughed and pointed at Jeremy, "when he finally pops the question."

Jeremy smirked and didn't say a word, and I wondered whether he was planning to ask Kenzie at some point. Their relationship was almost as intense as Bailey and Ryder's, and Jeremy absolutely adored Cole, Kenzie's son...with Chace. Still couldn't wrap my head around that whole situation. It was like daytime TV.

"And what if Ryder knocks Bailey up again?" Linc asked. "Then there'd be Cole, this baby, and another. There's always going to be Jones babies."

"You know what I mean." Indie sighed and threw her hands in the air. "This is the first baby for our group. Cole doesn't count—no offence, Kenz—

because he was a baby before we all knew about him. He's the big kid of the group. But this baby, this baby is the beginning of the future." Indie clapped and grinned.

"Ace, you okay? You're talking a lot of crap." Linc reached for her and pulled her close.

"Eh. Just been reading Bailey's baby books. But, you know, they're all philosophical and not useful."

Johnny started laughing. "Watch out, kid." He pointed at Linc. "You'll be next."

Indie just smiled, and I had a sneaking suspicion that Johnny was right. Indie would be next.

Linc's eyes focused on Indie, and he winked. "Don't mind practicing."

"Has anyone called the grandmothers?" Kenzie suddenly asked. Everyone looked at each other blankly. "Shit, I'll do it."

She left the room, and we all fell into silence. Surely, Ryder had texted them as well.

"How long does it take?" Linc asked after a while.

"You got a lot to learn, kid. We could be here all night," Johnny answered.

Linc paled.

Kenzie returned a minute later, huffing. "I can't believe she's here. What is she doing here?"

"Who?" Indie rushed to the door and poked her head out.

"Christina. She's out in the hall."

And that was the moment my phone buzzed in my pocket. Ignoring the sudden increase in chatter as the girls discussed all the reasons they hated Christina, I pulled it out to see a text.

Christina: Can you come outside? I don't want to go in there.

Audrey leaned over and read the text. "You can't go out there."

"I have to. You read it. She doesn't want to come in here. I can't expect her to face a room full of people who hate her. Besides, I'll have to drive her back to the school to pick up her car."

Audrey frowned. "Drop her off and come straight back?"

"Of course." I kissed the top of her head and left the room.

"Where's he going?" Indie's voice drifted into the hall.

"He'll be back soon," was all Audrey said, and I smiled, knowing she wasn't going to throw me under the bus and tell them what I was really doing. What would they all think if they knew about Christina and me? They'd be pissed. But then again, I didn't really care. I liked them as a group. They were cool, fun to hang around, but they were Audrey's family, not mine. In the end, what they thought of me didn't matter. Audrey's opinion was the only one I cared about.

I found Christina at the reception desk, tapping her blood red nails on the counter, waiting for me.

She gave me a nervous smile as I approached. "Thank you. I saw Kenzie and freaked out. I'd be the last person they'd want to see."

I nodded and put my hands in my pockets because I had the urge to reach for her and comfort her. I knew she screwed up when she was younger, but who didn't? I also knew the person she was now and believed if everyone in that waiting room tried to get to know her, they might find she was pretty cool and not as much of a bitch as they thought. "I'll take you back to your car," I said.

"Oh, umm, okay. Thanks." She fidgeted with the strap on her bag. "I have Bailey's stuff too."

My gaze followed hers to the ground where Bailey's things were packed neatly into a box.

"I cleared out her desk and brought her bag and things too."

"Thanks." I reached down and picked it up. "I'll just go and give it to Indie."

I walked back into the waiting room.

"That was quick." Audrey's face lit up.

"Yeah, I ran into Ms. Brown. She'd brought all Bailey's things, so Bailey doesn't have to worry about going back and packing up her stuff with the baby, or whatever." I raised an eyebrow at Audrey as if to say, "*See, she can be nice.*"

"Hmmm. Probably just wanted the desk and locker for herself. She's selfish enough that she would have cleaned it out straightaway." Indie scoffed. "She never does anything out of the kindness of her heart."

I shook my head and walked out. There was no getting through to them. They'd made up their minds about her, and there was nothing anyone could do to change that.

CHAPTER THIRTEEN

Christina

I watched Bennett out of the corner of my eye as he drove us silently back toward the school. I wanted to talk to him, but I didn't know what to say. The fact he didn't make me walk into that room with everyone there proved he cared about my feelings in some way. If he didn't, he wouldn't have come to me.

"How was Bailey doing?"

"Don't know. We hadn't heard anything. It's just a waiting game." His hands tightened on the steering wheel, the muscles in his arms contracting.

"How do you know them all?" I was genuinely curious how he became friends with them. He was much younger, and it didn't make much sense. I was surprised when he lifted Bailey into his arms earlier and took care of her. Any other student probably wouldn't have done such a thing.

He was a good guy, and it only made me want him more. It was going to be a long ten weeks. Nine weeks. One week had passed torturously slow. Nine more weeks to go, and maybe we could pick up where we left off.

"Audrey."

Of course. It always came back to Audrey.

I tried not to show my disappointment and waited for him to explain.

"After the fire, Audrey had no one. She was orphaned. Nate and Indie's parents took her in, cared for her, and sought the best medical treatment money could buy to help her."

"The fire was that bad?"

Bennett laughed darkly. "Yeah, it was bad. It killed her parents and her sister. Nearly took her life as well. If it weren't for Nate and Brody finding her in the rubble when they did, she wouldn't be here today."

"I had no idea. She's strong."

I felt terrible for the girl, knowing more of the story.

"She's a fighter. The strongest person I know."

"How did you become friends?"

He concentrated on the road, but his posture tensed. "We started school the same day. Neither of us wanted to be there, and we both took refuge in Bailey's classroom." He smiled at a memory. "Audrey was hiding under Bailey's desk, too nervous to face the students because of her anxiety. She was worried what they'd think of her, or that they'd stare at her and be cruel. We became best friends instantly."

"What about y—"

Bennett held up at hand to cut me off. "What's

111

with the sudden interest in my personal life?"

I took a deep breath and turned in my seat as Bennett pulled his car up beside mine in the parking lot. I lifted a shoulder. "I want to get to know you better?"

"Is that a question, or are you telling me?"

"I'm telling you."

"Why?"

"Look, I know I've been petty and jealous."

Bennett smirked. "Go on."

"And I don't deserve to even have you talk to me, but I like you. I shouldn't, because you're my student, and it would cause all sorts of trouble if anything were to happen."

"But?"

"There is no but. That's it. I like you. I want to know you better."

"But...we still have nine weeks of you being my teacher, and nothing can come of this until then. You said so yourself."

"Right."

"So, where do you see this going in nine weeks' time?" He dropped his arm from the steering wheel and rested it on the console between us. His fingers hung dangerously close to my thigh.

"I don't know, but I'd like to find out. Wouldn't you?" I moved my leg closer to his hand, hoping he'd close the small distance and touch me. My body was buzzing with anticipation. It needed to feel him, and I'd take just about anything at the moment. Even his pinky finger that was drawing lazy circles above my knee.

He stared straight ahead into the shrubs that lined

the school parking lot.

Not a person was left.

The place was barren.

"What about Hamilton?" he asked.

"Who?" I was too focused on the light touch of his finger.

"Mr. Hamilton? The teacher who was all but under your skirt last night?" His voice was controlled, low, but I could sense the resentment. His jaw tightened.

"He's nothing. I wanted to make you jealous."

"I don't get jealous."

Unfortunately, I did.

"I tried to convince myself this was just a fling, that I didn't need you or want you," I said, my voice lowering as I spoke.

"Did it work?"

"Would I be sitting here hoping you'd do something more than caressing my knee with your little finger if it did?"

Bennett dropped his gaze to his hand. Lips tilted in a half smile, he flattened his palm and curled his fingers around the inside of my thigh. Leaning in, he spoke softly, and his breath whispered across my lips, he was that close. "And what more would you have me do?"

His tongue traced along his bottom lip as he dragged his hand slowly up the inside of my thigh. My heart was pounding a thousand beats a minute in my chest, so hard it rattled my rib cage. The anticipation was killing me. I wanted to scream at him to hurry up, to move his hand further. My fingers were aching to grab hold of the small bun at the back of his head and smash his mouth against mine. We were so close, and then...

"I should go." Bennett pulled away.

"What?" I shoved my hands against his chest and sat back. "You're kidding, right?"

"Look where we are, Christina. I will not be responsible for you losing your job, or worse, no matter how tempted I am to throw you in this back seat right now. I'm skating on thin ice as it is. If I get caught in a compromising position with my teacher, my father will ship me off to live with my mother faster than you can moan my name."

"You want to throw me in the back seat?" My eyes lit up at the thought even as I berated myself for getting so excited at the prospect.

"I want to do so much more than that."

I looked thoughtfully at the back seat, still wishing he'd just do what he wanted to with me, but I knew he was right.

"Nine weeks?"

"Nine weeks." He nodded.

"What do we do until then?"

"Nothing. Things will go on as normal."

"Bennett, how old are you?"

He smirked. "Old enough to be legal."

"Really?"

"We're sitting in my car, Christina," he pointed out with an amused expression.

"Shit," I hissed. "That was dumb. So, you're eighteen?"

"Met you the day after my eighteenth birthday, actually."

My eyes widened, and my mouth dropped open.

"I can't believe you're so young."

"I think I more than make up for it, don't you?"

"Yes," I breathed, leaning closer to him, and my lips parted of their own accord. Just a taste. One kiss wouldn't hurt, surely?

Bennett cleared his throat. "It's going to be a very long nine weeks if you keep looking at me like that, Ms. Brown."

"I'm going to be very wound up if you keep saying my name like that."

"You like when I call you Ms. Brown, huh? Kinky." He winked.

God, he was delectable. His blue eyes sparkled with life, and the dimple on his cheek flashed. He was the perfect specimen. I wanted to trace my nails down his back and lick a trail from his chest all the way dow—

He laughed. "Eyes are up here."

"Can't help myself."

"I should go." Bennett sighed and closed his eyes, tipping his head back against the seat. He swallowed, and the Adam's apple in his throat bobbed from the movement, and I may have groaned.

"Do you have to?"

"Baby's coming, I should be there." He opened his eyes and looked at me.

"Right." I nodded. "Well, I'll see you on Monday. Wish Bailey and Ryder all the best for me."

Bennett stared, shock crossing his features. "Really?"

"Sure. I have no issue with them anymore."

"Okay. Have a good weekend, Ms. Brown," he said with a playful smile as I climbed out of the car and stepped over to mine. "Hey!" He wound his window down, and I turned to look at him. "We should do this again."

"What?"

"Talk. I like talking to you."

"I'm not talking to you for nine weeks, Bennett, unless it's about your exams." I hopped in my car and closed the door, drowning out the sound of Bennett's laughter.

CHAPTER FOURTEEN

Bennett

My phone had buzzed with a text while I was trying not to get hot with Christina, but damn, she made it hard. In more ways than one.

I grabbed my phone and checked the message.

Audrey: Where are you?

My stomach sank. I promised Audrey I'd stay away from Christina, and I would…for the next nine weeks. After that, all bets were off. But I felt terrible now because I'd have to lie to her, and that was the last thing I wanted to do. She was my bro, and we didn't lie. But I knew I couldn't tell her about the arrangement Christina and I just made because she wouldn't understand.

She had Brody, and he was perfect, and everyone loved him. They were made for each other. Everyone hated Christina, and I understood why. She treated Bailey like shit, though I still hadn't got

Christina's version of the story. But the wolf pack, as Audrey liked to call them, were all very close and protective of one another. They'd included me in their little gang because I was Audrey's friend, and I knew they'd take it personally if they found out about Christina.

For now, I had to keep my mouth shut and pretend like nothing was going on.

Bennett: Coming now.

I pulled out of the parking lot and rushed to the hospital, wondering whether Bailey'd had the baby yet.

The waiting room was full when I walked in. Nate and Brody had arrived, and so had Ryder's and Bailey's mothers. Kenzie's son Cole was playing with Jeremy in the corner, and everyone else was sitting around looking bored out of their brains.

"No baby yet?" I asked when I took a seat next to Audrey.

"Not yet." She yawned and stretched.

"Want a coffee?" I offered. I didn't really want to sit around and do nothing.

She nodded. "I'll come with you. Anyone else want a coffee?"

"Oh, I'll have a packet of gummy worms!" Indie said.

"And I'll have an iced tea," Kenzie called out.

"No one wants coffee? Great! I won't get anything, then." Audrey smiled before anyone else could shout out orders. "Brody?"

"Please."

She leaned down and kissed him. "Won't be long."

He looked at me, his eyebrows pinched together, and I thought he was going to say something, but he didn't. He turned back to Linc and continued their conversation.

We walked out into the hall, and Audrey took a deep breath. "It was getting stuffy in there."

"There were a lot of people," I agreed.

"How come it took you so long to come back?" She posed her question innocently, but I knew she was suspicious. What could I say? That I almost felt up our English teacher in the school parking lot? Or that we agreed to stay away from each other until the end of the year, and then it was no holds barred?

"Oh, uh…Christina's car wouldn't start. I had to jump start it for her."

Lie.

Total lie. And I hoped Audrey didn't question me on it.

"Oh. Good. I thought that, you know, maybe things got a little…" She trailed off and waved a hand between us.

"Sexy?"

"Ewww, no. God. I know you're not that dumb to pursue her anymore."

My heart sank. She had total faith in me, and I was lying to her face. Great best friend I was.

"I was going to say nasty. Because, well, she's a bi—"

"Bitch. Yeah, so everyone keeps saying. Whatever. It's fine. You have nothing to worry about, okay?"

"Good. It's only because I care."

"I know, and I love you for it." I wrapped her in my arms and kissed her head.

"Angel face!" a voice called down the hallway.

Audrey chuckled as she pulled away and turned to face the guy coming toward us. "I was wondering how long it would take for him to get here."

"Am I late? Did I miss it?" He swept Audrey into his arms and spun her around.

"Hi, Jack. No, you haven't missed anything. We're still waiting." She stumbled slightly when he dropped her to her feet.

His eyes shifted to me, and he fixed his hair and tried to give what I imagined would be a sexy smile. "Hi, handsome."

"Jack," I laughed. I'd met him a few times and liked the guy. He was a bit much to take at first, but once you got to know him, you realised he was probably one of the best guys you could meet.

"Come here often?"

"No. Yourself?"

"No, but I might start if you're here."

"You are not hitting on my friend, Jack." Audrey slapped his arm.

"Sorry, angel face, but are you sure you have the right man? I mean, you chose Brody. Don't you want to maybe get an upgrade? A younger model. Newer. Faster." Jack tilted his head and looked me up and down. "More powerful. Built to last."

"Oh, my god. Can't take you anywhere." She grabbed Jack's shoulders and turned him in the direction of the waiting room. "In there. Go!"

"I'll just go and keep your boyfriend distracted,

Audrey, in case you want to take Bennett for a test drive!" Jack cackled as he walked away with a bounce in his step.

"He's so embarrassing." Audrey buried her face in her hands.

"Want a test drive?" I teased as Jack sauntered down the hall with extra sway in his hips.

"What? No!"

"One day." I nudged her with my elbow, but she just rolled her eyes and ignored my comment.

"Come to find me later, handsome," Jack called back to me.

"I don't think you can handle me," I said, trying not to laugh when he came to a stop.

"Is that a challenge?" His eyes lit, and a wicked grin spread across his face.

"No, Jack. It's not a challenge," Audrey said before turning and poking me in the chest. "And you, stop encouraging him."

"Later, baby." Jack blew a kiss and walked into the waiting room.

"He's unbelievable."

"He's fun. Come on, bro, let's go and get everyone a coffee."

I grabbed Audrey's hand and led her to the cafeteria. We didn't bother ordering what they had asked for but bought enough coffee for everyone and a juice for Cole, then carried it all back to the waiting room.

"Oh, thank god." Indie groaned and snatched a tray from my hands to distribute the coffee.

Ryder's and Bailey's mums were grateful. They both looked so nervous and excited about the baby.

It wasn't even that late, but sitting around with nothing to do was surprisingly exhausting.

My phone buzzed in my pocket again, and I pulled it out to read the message, smiling when I saw it. She actually cared.

Christina: Any news yet?

Bennett: Not yet. Will keep you updated.

Christina: You don't have to. I was just curious.

Bennett: Shut up. I will. You obviously want to know.

Christina: Maybe a little bit.

I smiled to myself and put my phone back in my pocket. I looked up to see Audrey's eyes focused on me.

"What?"

"Who was that?"

I lifted my shoulders and swallowed the bad taste in my mouth as I spoke. "A friend."

Lie.

Total lie.

And she knew it too. She was my only real friend, apart from Chris, but he was off the grid for a while, trying to get his act cleaned up.

"He's allowed to have other friends, cupcake," Brody reassured her and wrapped his arm around her waist.

I lifted an eyebrow and waited for her to challenge me again, but she kept quiet and turned her focus to Brody. Which left me with Jack. At least he was entertaining and made the time pass.

Kenzie and Jeremy left to get Cole some dinner after everyone realised it was going to be a long night, and the rest of us sat silently staring at the clock but not making time go faster.

"Hey, Jack?" Linc said after a while and rubbed his hands over his arms.

"Yeah?"

"You got a jacket in your car?"

Jack tapped his chin. "That depends."

"On what?"

"Are you going to wear it, or is it for Indie?"

"Me. I'm freezing because Ace wouldn't let me get changed."

Indie gave him an innocent smile. "I didn't want to miss anything."

"We've been here for hours, and nothing's happened."

"Stupid ass," she muttered under her breath. She called him that a lot. I didn't understand it, but apparently it wasn't really an insult. A term of endearment, according to Bailey.

"Sorry. No jacket. Guess you'll have to freeze or let me warm you up." Jack smiled sweetly.

Linc rolled his eyes and pulled Indie to his chest, wrapping his arms around her. "That's what Ace is for."

"Suit yourself." Jack waved him off.

"Jack?"

"Yes, babycakes?"

123

I swore he had a nickname for everyone.

"If you give Linc a jacket, his naked chest will touch it. Think about that. You can wear something that Linc's firm body has felt," Indie said, a playful smile on her face as she rubbed her hands over Linc's chest.

Jack's eyes followed the movement, and his mouth hung open. "I'll be right back!"

He ran out of the room.

"That wasn't uncomfortable at all," Linc grumbled.

Indie buried her head in Linc's chest and giggled. "He's too easy."

Jack returned with a jacket, faster than anyone expected him to. His face was flushed, his breaths hard and fast. Looked like he'd just run a marathon. "Here."

"Thanks, man." Linc took the jacket and shrugged it on. "Ah, so much better." He screwed his nose up. "Jesus, did you drown it in cologne?"

"No, but thank you. I'll take the compliment. No one has ever called me Jesus before. And, of course. I smell enticing. Is it enticing you?"

"It's giving me a headache." Linc sneezed.

"Give it back, then?" Jack held out his hand.

"No."

"Well—"

Jack was cut off by Ryder walking into the waiting room, his eyes wide and in shock.

"Holy fuck. I'm a dad," he announced. And before anyone could even stand and congratulate him, he turned and ran back out of the room.

It was silent. The guys all stood there with the

same expression Ryder had on his face. Pure shock. Like they couldn't believe it actually happened. They had a baby. And the girls all had tears streaming down their cheeks.

After a moment, cheers erupted, and there were hugs and kisses and more tears and a room full of celebration.

It was a sight to see. The way all these people cared for each other and supported each other was incredible, and I couldn't even get my dad to remember my birthday.

The door opened again, and the room fell silent.

Ryder stood there with a tiny bundle in his arms.

"I have a daughter," he whispered, staring down at her with all the adoration in the world. A small smile appeared on his face. "Meet Sage."

Cue the shocked stares and tears again as everyone crowded around him and Sage.

"Her name is perfect," Kenzie said.

"She's beautiful." Bailey's mum pushed her way through.

"Congratulations," Jeremy said.

Audrey stood on her toes to get a better look. "She's so sweet."

"I love her already," Jack gushed.

"How's Bailey?" Nate asked.

"She's good. She's in recovery but will be out soon, and you can all see her."

"Can I hold her?" Indie asked.

"Get your own. She's mine. And no fucker's getting their hands on her." Ryder hugged her closer, making everyone laugh.

"She hasn't even opened her eyes yet, and he's

already planning the death of the first boy she kisses." Kenzie laughed.

"Poor kid," Brody said.

"There will be no boys until she's forty." Ryder said it with such complete seriousness, and I fully believed it.

Then he smiled when he saw Indie's frown. "No, I have to get her back. She needs bonding time with Bailey before anyone else can hold her. But you can all fight over her soon." He kissed Indie on the cheek and cradled Sage closer to his body, protective, as everyone either kissed him or clapped a hand on his back in congratulations, and then they were gone.

The room fell silent again until Linc broke it. "Hey, Ace," he whispered loudly. "Wanna make a baby?"

"Right now?"

He looked around the room at everyone staring at them. "That's a little too kinky for me, but maybe we can practice when we get home?"

Indie nodded. "Practice makes perfect."

CHAPTER FIFTEEN

Christina

Bennett had messaged Friday night to tell me Bailey had a baby girl, and that Ryder was already overprotective. I expected nothing less of him. And I was truly happy for them.

Now it was Monday, and I stood facing the double doors, trying to work up the courage to possibly do the most daring, daunting thing I could think of.

With the bag in my hand, I walked inside the building and over to the reception desk.

"I'm here to see Bailey Jones." I smiled at the nurse.

"You know Bailey?" The nurse frowned at me. There was something familiar about her, but I couldn't work out what it was. Something in her face. She reminded me of someone.

"Yes. Uh…we're colleagues and old school friends," I answered politely and wondered what was with the inquisition. Couldn't she just give me the damn room number and let me go?

"Sorry, what was your name? I need to put you in the register." Her green eyes scrutinised my face.

"Christina Brown."

She chewed on her bottom lip and thought about it for a moment. "I know who you are."

"Yes, because I just told you."

"You put my girl through hell in high school."

"Your girl?"

"Bailey."

"You're Bailey's mum?"

"No, Ryder's." She scowled, and it became so apparent. The curly hair, the green eyes, the dimples. She was an older version of her son.

I took a deep breath and tried again. "I'm sorry for any pain I caused back then. I was young and stupid and naïve. I'm trying to be better and want to make things right with Bailey and Ryder. That's why I'm here."

She studied me and leaned in, pressing a finger to my chest. "Fine. But if she wants you to leave, then you go, and don't let me see your face again. Understand?"

I nodded.

Now I understood where Ryder got his intimidation skills. Mumma Jones was powerful.

"She's in room twenty-seven. Down the hall and to the right."

"Thank you."

I took cautious steps toward Bailey's room, trying to delay the inevitable. I knew I was doing the right thing, but it didn't make it any easier to do. How could I even begin to make up for the hell I'd put her through?

I took a deep breath and steeled my nerves before knocking on the door.

"Come in," she called softly.

I pushed open the door gently and stepped into the room. It was full of pink. And balloons and teddy bears. It looked like the gift shop had been set up beside Bailey's bed.

I glanced down at my bag and frowned. My gift seemed pathetic compared to the rest of the stuff filling the room.

"Christina?" Ryder stood and put his hands in his pockets. "What the hell do you want?"

"Jones, it's okay," Bailey said in a soothing voice. She already sounded like a mother.

"Umm, I..." I was stuck for words. I never had a problem saying what was on my mind, but right then, I couldn't form a sentence. "I bought a gift. And wanted to say congratulations."

Bailey smiled and shifted the baby in her arms. "That's very sweet. Thank you."

I shrugged and stood there, unsure what to do next.

"Umm, come in. Don't stand in the door," Bailey offered.

I walked further into the room and placed the gift beside her bed. "She's beautiful."

"Would you like to hold her?"

I stared at her, wide-eyed. She was offering to let me hold her child. I couldn't believe it. I had walked in there half expecting to be kicked out immediately. It wouldn't have surprised me if she had. Actually, I'd probably have felt more

129

comfortable if she'd told me to leave and not come back, then I wouldn't have to make an effort. I could say I tried and failed and just move on.

I looked at Ryder. His arms were crossed, and his jaw was tense. He liked the idea of me holding his child no more than I did.

"No, it's okay. I should go. I just wanted to say congratulations." I pointed to the door and stepped back.

"Christina, you came all the way down here, when we both know you didn't have to. It's okay to stay. Here." She shifted on the bed and held out her daughter, the most precious thing in the world to both of them, for me to take.

So, I did.

I took the small bundle of pink in her arms and cradled her to my chest. I was sure I heard Ryder growl as his baby wriggled in my arms. Her eyes fluttered open, and she yawned, the tiniest, cutest yawn I'd ever seen. I smiled at her in awe; I couldn't help it. "She's amazing."

"Thank you."

"What's her name?"

"Sage."

"I should have known it would be something spiritual and strong. It's perfect." I looked at Ryder. "She looks like you."

He didn't speak. He nodded, the hard expression from before softening a touch.

I cuddled Sage for a little while longer, mesmerised by her facial expressions, before handing her back to Bailey. "Thank you for letting me hold her."

"That's okay. Thank you for coming."

"I wanted to." I shrugged, suddenly realising I did, in fact, want to be there. My original thought had been to go and apologise because I wanted to be a better person. Selfishly, I only wanted to be better for Bennett. I wanted to be worthy of him, and in order to do that, I had to make amends with the past.

That was why I went to the hospital.

For Bennett.

But as I stood there holding Sage, something shifted. Just a small shift, nothing alarming, but it was strong enough to make me realise I really did want to be better. For myself. For everyone.

I didn't want to be the selfish bitch no one liked.

I looked at Ryder and the way he loved his family, and I wanted something like that one day.

I thought about Indie and how she stood by Bailey through all the hell and worse that Chace and I had put her through. And I wanted a friend like that.

I thought about Bennett and how he would go to the ends of the Earth for Audrey. And I wanted that.

I wanted someone to care about me and look at me like I was the most important person in the world. And I'd never have that if I continued the way I had been.

It was time to turn over a new leaf.

"I appreciate it."

"Well, I really should go," I said. "Let you get some rest. Thank you for the cuddles."

"Anytime." Bailey smiled. "And thank you for the gift."

"It was nothing."

I gave an awkward wave and walked out, closing the door behind me. I slumped against the wall and took a deep breath, trying to calm my nerves.

The door opened, and Ryder walked out.

"Can I talk to you?"

"O-okay." I stammered.

He walked away, not bothering to see if I would follow—which, of course, I did.

"I don't know what you're doing, why you're here being nice all of a sudden, and I don't care. I appreciate that you got Bailey to the hospital on Friday, but other than that, I don't care. You know how kind Bailey is. She'd give the shirt off her back to anyone who needed it. I don't want her taken for a ride again. So, I'm going to say this once, and once only." He paused to make sure I was listening before he continued. "Bailey is very forgiving. More so now than when we were younger. She looks at the world in a different way. She sees the good in people. And for some fucking reason, she sees good in you. Don't screw it up. If you want to make nice, be sure you mean it. Don't take advantage of her or mistake her kindness for weakness, or I will end you. Remember, you're not only messing with her, but my whole family, and I won't take that lying down."

He didn't even give me a chance to respond before he turned on his heel and walked back to the room.

"Ryder?" I called. My voice was croaky and caught in my throat. "I won't screw it up. I really am sorry."

"I'm not the one you have to say that to." He leaned against the door to Bailey's room.

"That's where you're wrong. By hurting Bailey, I hurt you too, and I'm sorry."

"So, prove it." He pushed the door open with his back and disappeared into the room with his family.

I left the hospital and drove aimlessly around town, unsure what I wanted to do. I could go home and open a bottle of wine, put on reno shows, and relax. Or I could go back to the school and do some work. Get ahead in my planning and make sure everything was ready for the students now that Bailey was well and truly gone. Neither of those two options appealed to me, though.

I knew what I wanted to do. And I also knew it was stupid.

In the end, I decided on a drink at the bar attached to the roadhouse. After Ryder's little threat and the shitstorm that was my life, I felt like I deserved a drink to unwind. It was almost five o'clock, so that was good enough for me.

The bar looked entirely different in the light of day. The other night, I hadn't noticed how retro the décor was or how much it had changed since the last time I came here in high school.

The same angry-looking bartender was there again. I wondered whether he had a perpetual scowl on his face, or if it was only me that bought out that side of him. He looked perfectly cheery talking with Bailey and Ryder the other night.

"Whiskey. Neat." I gave him my best smile as I pulled up a stool.

"What do you want?" He crossed his arms and

frowned.

"Whiskey?" I repeated slowly, unsure of what he meant.

He poured my drink and slid it over to me. "This comes with a warning."

I raised my eyebrow and sat a little straighter. Who was this guy, and why did he think he had any right to talk to me that way, let alone give me a warning?

"Stay away from Bailey. Stay away from Kenzie."

"What's it to you?"

"I look after what's mine, and I know all about you Christina."

"Yours?"

"Kenzie. Cole. Mine." He leaned on the bar, his tattoo-covered forearms flexing under his weight.

"I don't want trouble. I promise."

"Keep it that way."

"Who are you?"

"Jeremy," he said and walked away, effectively ending our conversation.

Jeremy. Kenzie's boyfriend. That explained the open hostility.

Not wanting to stay somewhere I clearly wasn't welcome, I downed my drink and left. The old me would have sat there all night just to piss him off, but the new me, the me that was trying to make amends, knew when to quit.

CHAPTER SIXTEEN

Bennett

Seven weeks and two days to go.

The countdown was on, and it was the longest damn countdown of my life. It was nearly impossible to concentrate on anything in English other than ripping off those tight dresses Christina insisted on wearing and leaving her in nothing but her six-inch heels.

I was going to fail my exams because all I could think about was bending my English teacher over her desk and spanking her ass with the ruler I swore she was purposely stroking in such a way to make me incredibly uncomfortable.

She smirked, sensing my unease as I shifted in my seat and tried unsuccessfully to adjust my jeans.

"What is wrong with you?" Audrey hissed from beside me. "You're sweating. It's kind of gross."

"I think I'm getting sick," I lied. Again.

I'd been lying to her a lot the last couple of weeks. And it was getting harder to keep up the charade. Christina had stayed faithful to her word and acted like we were nothing to each other, except for those times she was sending me sexy little signals, like right then with the ruler, but she swore black and blue she wasn't doing anything when I questioned her on it. She'd told me repeatedly to stop thinking with my dick, and that it was only my imagination, and maybe it was, because no one else seemed to notice anything.

"So, you don't want to come and see Sage with me after school?" She sounded disappointed.

I wanted to tell her I'd go with her, but I'd stupidly just said I was sick, and if I was ill, I couldn't very well go and see the baby.

"I better not. Don't want to get her sick." Besides, I had to work again tonight, since Ryder was MIA because of Sage.

Lie.

"That's okay. Next time."

"Brody picking you up today?"

"Yeah, we're going to see Sage, and then we're going away for the weekend," she said excitedly.

"How come I didn't know about this?"

"You did. I've told you three times, and each time you asked why you didn't know." She bit her lip and raised an eyebrow and waited for an answer.

I winced. "Really?"

"Uh-huh."

I really was sucking in the friendship department lately, and I put it down to not wanting to lie to Audrey. I knew rationally I wasn't lying. Nothing was going on with Christina and me at the moment, but the second graduation was over, it was on. I wasn't putting myself through this torture for nothing.

"Sorry, bro."

"What's going on? You've been so distracted lately."

"Nothing. Everything is fine."

"How're things with your dad?"

"Wants me to go to the club with him tomorrow. Probably so he can chase the waitress again and have me there for a cover."

"Are you going?"

I shrugged.

"I have to. If I don't, he'll send me to my mother's."

"You're eighteen. Surely, he can't do that."

"No, probably not, but he can kick me out, and then where would I go?"

"Live with me?"

"Don't think Brody would be too keen on that idea."

Christina cleared her throat, and I looked up to see her standing in front of our table. Her eyes narrowed, she placed her hands on her slim hips and stood tall and straight. My eyes immediately followed the curves of her body and got stuck on her chest.

"Am I interrupting something?" she asked.

"Not at all, Ms. Brown," I said slowly, knowing she liked the way I spoke her name.

Ha. Maybe that'd teach her. She swallowed. The movement was slow and exaggerated. Her breath hitched.

"We were just discussing the worksheet,"

Audrey said and waved her sheet in front of her face.

"Well, I highly doubt weekend plans are included on your worksheet, Audrey."

Christina turned and walked back to the front of the room.

"Bitch," Audrey muttered. "Did you hear she's been talking to Bailey?"

"What?" My head snapped around to look at Audrey.

"Yeah. Apparently, she went to see Sage in the hospital and has been to visit Bailey at home. Bailey is nuts, and I can't believe Ryder would let that witch in their house."

That was interesting. I didn't think either of them had any intention of making things right again. Maybe I was wrong.

The bell sounded, so I helped Audrey pack up her stuff and then packed mine before standing to leave.

"Bennett, can I see you for a moment?" Christina called over the noise of the other students leaving the room.

Audrey's eyebrows pinched together, and her lips formed a pout.

I gave Audrey a shrug. I had no clue why Christina wanted to see me. Though I doubted it was to fulfil my ruler fantasy.

"Audrey, you may go." Christina pointed to the door. "This doesn't concern you."

"But," Audrey gasped. Her eyes widened, and she sucked in a breath.

Shit.

I knew that look.

I dropped our bags and scooped her up into my arms. Taking a seat on the table, I buried her head in my chest and rubbed her back.

Christina stood at the front of the room, watching curiously. She opened her mouth to speak but couldn't get the words out.

I knew what she was thinking.

"It's okay. Breathe in....and out. I'm here." I looked at Christina. "Get me my water bottle."

She rushed over to the bags at my feet and dug around in the pocket for my drink bottle. I took it from her and then pulled Audrey back. "Here, bro, drink this. It's okay." I put the straw to her lips, and she sipped slowly.

Her head fell against my chest again as she tried to regain her composure.

"Sorry, I didn't know."

"I walk her to all her classes, and when you told her to leave without me, she panicked." I shrugged. It had happened before when I had been late to meet her out the front of one of her classes. I had found her on the floor in a ball.

"I had no idea. Is she going to be okay?"

"I should take her home. It exhausts her. She'll go home and sleep now."

"Right, okay. I'll give you a pass, so you don't get detention."

"Wouldn't want that."

Christina returned to her desk and scribbled on a pad. "Take that, and if you have any trouble, tell them I said it was okay."

"Thanks, Ms. Brown." I smirked when she

139

gasped in a breath.

Helping Audrey to her feet once she'd calmed down, I grabbed both our bags and walked her out the door and to my car.

"I'm sorry," Audrey mumbled on the way back to the Kellerman house.

"What for?"

"Panicking again."

"You can't help it. It's not like you do it purposely." I reached over and grabbed her hand.

"I feel like such a loser. I mean, I can't even go to class alone without you holding my hand." She lifted our hands and shook them between us.

"You're not a loser."

"Can I tell you something?"

"Of course." I took a deep breath, not liking the tone in her voice. She sounded afraid.

"I panicked because I was scared."

I laughed. "I know."

"No, not scared to walk to class on my own. I really think I'm okay to do that now."

"Really? That's great." I smiled. That was enormous progress. If she could walk around the school on her own without fear of the other students, she was doing fantastic.

I was proud of her.

"Have you noticed my panic attacks have been worse these last few weeks?"

"I have. But you said it was because you were worried for me."

"I lied."

I pulled the car into her drive. "What?"

"I'm worried for you, but that's not why I have

140

the panic attacks."

"You're starting to scare me now. If you don't tell me soon, I might have a panic attack."

"They're caused because I'm afraid of losing you." She sniffed and wiped her nose on her sleeve.

"You won't lose me. I'm never going anywhere."

"But I already feel like I am."

I unbuckled her seatbelt and pulled her over to me, cradling her on my chest like a child.

"Why? Why do you feel like that?"

"Christina. She's always there, lingering in the background. And I know you said it was over, but I can't help but worry it won't stay over, and you'll leave me for her. It starts with keeping you back after class, so I have to walk by myself. Then it progresses to you not being able to pick me up for school in the morning. Or forgetting to video chat with me at night because you're busy with her." She cried. The tears flowed down her cheeks, and my heart hurt. I wanted to make her better, make her see she wasn't going to lose me. Convince her she had nothing to worry about. "I can't lose you, Bennett. I've lost so much, and I won't lose you too."

"I won't leave you for her. I promise. We're bros. Remember. Bros before hos. And I'd never forget to call you."

"It won't always be like that, Bennett. One day you'll have a girlfriend, and she won't like me being in the picture and won't want me around. I mean what person in their right mind would be okay with our friendship? It's borderline dependant and not at all healthy."

"Says who?"

"My therapist."

"Fuck your therapist. I'm great with our friendship. Are you?"

She nodded and gave me a watery smile.

"Is Brody?"

She giggled quietly before it turned to tears. "Yeah, he is. He might not like this physical closeness too much, but he knows it's not romantic."

"You mean, he wouldn't like you sitting on my lap right now, in a cramped car, crying while I rubbed your back."

"No, but he'd understand and wouldn't worry about it."

"Then why are you?"

"Because Brody is one of a kind. No other person would be that okay with this. With us."

"If they're not okay with this, then fuck them too. I want nothing to do with them."

"It really doesn't worry you?"

"Not at all." How could I make her see that she was more important to me than anyone else? More important than any possible girlfriend. More important than Christina.

"It doesn't bother you what people think of us. I mean, Brody is my boyfriend, but to the outside world, so are you. The entire school thinks we're dating."

"If we were dating, there'd be a hell of a lot more of you moaning my name than crying," I joked, wanting to get her to smile again.

She slapped me in the chest.

"Who cares what everyone thinks? Sure, we're practically dating without the sexual benefits. Feel free to throw them on the table at any time, but it's got nothing to do with anything. I love you. More than anything. In a completely platonic, non-romantic way. You're my best friend, and I would lay down my life for you without blinking. So, stop worrying. You're stuck with me forever."

She hugged me, wrapped her arms around my neck as tight as she could. "How'd I get so lucky?"

"Because you've been through hell, and you deserve all the luck now."

"I love you, bestie."

I groaned. "I thought we had this conversation. Bros. We're bros."

"I like besties better."

I kissed her head. "Come on. Let's go watch a movie and fall asleep."

"Sounds good."

CHAPTER SEVENTEEN

Christina

The last thing I wanted to do on my Saturday afternoon was spend it at the club with John Sawyer and my father while they drank brandy and talked about who knew what.

But there I sat, in my pretty blue and white tennis dress, sipping lemonade with my father while we waited for Bennett's dad to arrive.

"How's work, sweetheart?"

"Great." I forced a smile.

"John treating you well?"

"Sure. We don't have a lot to do with each other." Not now, after he unsuccessfully tried to touch my ass last week as he followed me into the staff room. I'd managed to grab his hand and twist his fingers until he cried out in pain. The guy was a sleaze, and I couldn't see how he spawned someone as great as Bennett. They were complete opposites.

144

"Sorry we're late," John's voice boomed from behind me.

We're? I turned slowly, hoping not to see the one person I really did want to see. "Bennett drags his feet. He's like a petulant child sometimes."

Bennett's jaw twitched, and his eyes darkened. He looked about ready to punch his father, and I wouldn't blame him if he did.

"Bennett, good to see you, son." My dad smiled and shook Bennett's hand. "Sit down. Can I get you a drink?"

"That'd be great. Just a soda, thanks." Bennett smiled an easy, carefree smile before levelling me with his gaze. "Ms. Brown."

My throat felt thick, and my body trembled. He just had to call me that in front of our parents, one of whom was the school principal and my boss. I smiled. "We're out of school now, Bennett. You can save the formalities and call me Christina."

Bennett raised both hands, palm up, and shrugged. "Sorry, Ms. Brown, no can do. I was raised to show respect."

The smartass winked. I cleared my throat and picked up my lemonade and gulped it down.

"Thirsty?" He smirked.

"A little." I held his gaze, not wanting to back down from a challenge. I wasn't going to let him get to me.

"How's my daughter been treating you, Bennett?" My dad interrupted our unspoken conversation.

"She's treated me very well. Gone above and beyond to make things interesting...in class.

145

English is my favourite subject, actually, and," Bennett lifted his hand to me, eyes still focused on mine, "Ms. Brown really knows her stuff. She's quite proficient and has a great understanding of the work involved. She pushes the right buttons, challenges…us, and uses such creative energy that I can't get enough. I find myself studying every day." His tongue swept over his bottom lip. "Thirsty for knowledge and everything she is willing to teach."

"Wow! Hear that, sweetheart? You're quite the teacher. You might just increase your overall academic average next year, John," my dad bellowed proudly.

Meanwhile, I squirmed in my seat, suddenly feeling very hot and uncomfortable, desperately needing some buttons of my own pushed. I drained my drink and called the waiter for another one.

***

After a delicious lunch, I was preparing to leave and wanting to put some distance between Bennett and me before I gave in to temptation and straddled his lap in the dining room, when John cleared his throat. "All right. Why don't you two kids go for a wander around the club, entertain yourselves for a bit? We've got to talk a bit of shop." He gestured to my father, and I wondered what on earth type of business they could be discussing.

Bennett raised his eyebrows and shrugged. "Ms. Brown, want to play a game?"

He tilted his head in the direction of the court, but the playful smile on his lips told me tennis was not the game he intended to play.

"Maybe later. How about a walk around the grounds?"

"Sure. I'd like to pick your brain about the book we've been reading, *Dangerous Liaisons*, if you don't mind?" He schooled his features into an innocent expression.

That was not on our reading list.

"Not at all. If you'll excuse us, we'll give you some privacy." I smiled at my father and John before standing and following Bennett out of the dining room.

"That was fun. Don't you think?" he asked when we were away from people.

"What? Are you trying to get us busted?"

"There's nothing to bust." He tilted his head and dragged his gaze slowly down my body. "Well, not in that way."

"You're going to get us in trouble. Come on." I walked off, leading him further into the grounds, through the gardens, the maze, past the fountain, to the back corner where not many people ever ventured. It was shielded from the view of the main house by the maze and the giant evergreen trees.

I leaned my back against one of those trees, and Bennett came to stand in front of me. "Are we going to have a dangerous liaison, Ms. Brown?"

He leaned in and placed his hands on my hips, and I'd have been lying if I said I didn't react at all. My body acted on its own and arched into him.

I placed a hand on his chest. His very firm chest. The same chest that starred in my dreams again last night. My fingers spread out, and the thumping of his heart told me he was just as excited, or nervous, as I was.

No.

We couldn't do this. It wasn't right. We'd been doing well. And with barely seven weeks to go, I didn't want to ruin it now. I pushed on his chest.

A low rumble echoed in his throat. "I don't know if I can last another seven weeks." He buried his face in my shoulder, and I knew I needed to push him away, make him wait another seven weeks, but his breath on my neck gave me chills, and then he spoke again. "Just one taste."

I didn't move. I didn't say yes. I didn't say no. I waited in anticipation for his next move. My nerves were on high alert, and I felt every brush of his fingers on my waist, every whisper of his breath on my skin, every scratchy piece of bark digging into my back. And then his tongue…

The things he could do with his tongue.

He swept it across my collarbone, dragged it slowly up my neck. My head fell to the side, allowing him better access until he pulled my earlobe into his mouth with his teeth.

My eyes rolled back into my head, and I moaned, enjoying every sensation flowing through my body, right down to the tips of my toes.

"Bennett." I managed to find my voice. "You have to stop." I pushed his chest gently, not really trying to stop him at all, even though I knew I should.

"Don't want to," he whispered against my ear, sending a shiver down my spine.

"We can't," I said more firmly, and he backed

148

away.

"You're right. Seven weeks is a long time, though." He ran his hands through my hair and took four steps back, putting a considerable distance between us.

"It will be worth it, I promise."

His eyes lit up, and he groaned. "That's not fair. That just made it harder."

I laughed. I loved that he wanted this as much as I did. I only hoped it wasn't because it was forbidden. I wondered if when the time came, and I was no longer his teacher, he'd lose interest.

He sat on the grass under the tree opposite me and crossed his legs at the ankles. Arms behind his head, he leaned back and closed his eyes. His biceps bulged, and I wanted to throw caution to the wind and climb on his lap. But common sense prevailed. Barely.

I sank to the ground and watched him.

"Stop staring," he said.

"I'm not."

"Are too. It's creepy."

I laughed, and he suddenly sat straight up and looked me in the eye.

"We need to talk," he said. His serious tone made me nervous.

"I don't like the sound of that."

"It's not bad, but you need to know a few things if this is going to continue after graduation."

I folded my legs under me and picked at a blade of grass, twirling it between my fingers. "I'm listening."

"Audrey."

149

"I'm sorry about yesterday. Really." And I was. I never expected her to react that way to a simple request. I was starting to see the true effects the fire had on her, the more time I spent teaching her.

"I know, and that's sort of what this is about."

"Okay," I said slowly, confused as to what he was talking about.

"She's strong, a fighter, but she's also fragile."

"Got that." I nodded.

"She's also the most important person in my life. She's my best friend. Pretty much my only one." He paused and took a deep breath.

"I understand."

"You don't. Our friendship is…" he searched for the right words, "complicated, and different to most. We've grown closer than what friends normally would."

"You love her." It was a statement, not a question, as it suddenly dawned on me how strong his feelings for her were. I swallowed the lump in my throat and pressed a hand to my stomach to ease the queasy feeling. I was his second choice. He wanted me only because the girl he loved was off limits.

"I do. But, not like that. Not anymore, anyway. It's platonic, I swear, but the fact remains, Audrey comes first. Always. You need to be prepared to share me with her. Don't ever make me choose, because I can guarantee I won't choose you or anyone else over her."

His admission hit me like a tonne of bricks, square in the chest.

He'd always choose her.

150

Over me.

Over anyone else.

Audrey always came first.

It wasn't something I was prepared to hear. It wasn't something I was sure I could be okay with.

I liked Bennett, more than I should, and the thought of him being more invested in his friendship with Audrey than me hurt.

I nodded, wondering for the hundredth time what was so special about this girl that she managed to capture his heart and his undying loyalty. "Right. Well, it's not like this thing between us would ever get more serious than sex anyway, so it doesn't matter." I shrugged, hoping he wouldn't see the hurt I was feeling.

"Don't be like that. It's not that bad. Honestly."

"You just said you'd never choose anyone over her. How can I compete with that? How can I be okay with that?"

"I'm just putting it out there. Trying to be honest. She's the biggest part of my life. And if we're to pursue this in seven weeks, like I really fucking want to, I want you to be aware. We spend a lot of time together. Talk every night. If Brody isn't around and she needs someone, I'm the first one there, always."

"I get it. But I don't know if I'm okay with that."

Bennett folded his hands in his lap. "Well, there's seven weeks for you to decide what you want to do. Until then, I won't bring it up again."

"Okay." I stood and brushed the grass off the back of my skirt. "Are we done?" I wanted to leave. To put some distance between us. I was trying to be a better person, someone who deserved his affection, and he tells me I'll never be that because Audrey is so fucking perfect.

Bennett stood as well and rocked on his feet. "I guess."

"Good." I turned to walk away when he called my name again. Closing my eyes, I prepared myself for whatever other rubbish he could start talking about.

His fingers wrapped around my wrist, and he tugged me to face him. His hands were in my hair, and before I could take a breath, his mouth was on mine, moving roughly and passionately as his tongue explored my mouth. Against my better judgement, I melted under his touch, my hands grabbing at his shirt, trying to pull him closer when there was no space left between us. He backed me into the tree, his hands moving down my body until he lifted my legs around his waist.

My skin was on fire, my nerves on edge as we kissed, hidden from the view of our parents and the rest of the club. It was so wrong but felt so right. My body responded to his barest touch in a way that had never happened before. His lips peppered kisses down my throat until I grabbed his ponytail and pulled his mouth back to mine.

We were explosive together. Things between us could be phenomenal, but I couldn't share him with another girl. The thought of Audrey immediately stamped out any feelings I was having like a bucket of cold water on my head. I broke the kiss and untangled my legs from his waist.

Bennett set me down gently and took a step

back. Flushed cheeks, rapid breaths. He was just as turned on as I was, only I had the sense to stop it. Not before I lost my job, but before I lost my heart, which I quickly realised, as I watched the man before me, I was already in danger of doing.

"What was that?" I growled and shoved him away.

"A pretty spectacular kiss."

"Why?"

"Just in case you want nothing to do with me in seven weeks." He shrugged. "See you around, Ms. Brown." And then he walked away from me.

Probably straight to Audrey.

CHAPTER EIGHTEEN

Bennett

Five weeks to go.

It was only five weeks until graduation. Work was flat out, but I was enjoying it. I liked working on the cars—it gave me a sense of accomplishment when I fixed something—and I even helped out behind the bar when Jeremy got desperate. Ryder showed his face now and then, but not nearly as much as he used to. The preparation for exams was getting more intense. I tried to focus on my studies, but I struggled. English was the hardest. Obviously. For more than one reason.

I wondered if Christina was messing with me on purpose. Those tight dresses seemed to get tighter and shorter. Her heels got taller. And her lips got more and more blood red as the days went on.

"You'll never guess what I saw last night," Audrey said as she climbed into my car. I was taking her to Storm Cove for the day. It was Saturday, and Brody was working, so we were going to hang out and eat ice cream.

"Before or after we talked on the phone?"

"Umm. Before."

"And you're only telling me now?"

"Yes. Because I didn't know how you'd react. You've been quiet lately, and I wasn't sure whether that was good or bad. So, I wanted to tell you to your face."

My hands tightened on the steering wheel. "What?"

"Christina with Mr. Hamilton. I guess they're, like, dating now," she said slowly, her voice barely a whisper.

"Good for her," I ground out. My fingers tightened, and I was afraid I'd crush the steering wheel if I squeezed any harder. I guessed that settled it, then.

I was counting down for nothing.

"Really? You don't care?"

"We had sex, Audrey. Not a relationship. And it ended five weeks ago. It was nothing."

"I just thought…"

"Nope. Don't care. In fact, I have a date tonight as well."

Lie.

I really needed to stop lying to her.

"You do?"

"Yes."

"With who?" Her eyes lit up, and she smiled. "Tell me it's not someone from school, though, please."

155

"No, of course not. Ummm…" I searched my brain for a girl I knew who I could possibly convince to go on a date with me tonight. How pathetic was that? I was trying to find a girl I had no interest in to go on a date, to make my English teacher jealous. "Maya."

"Who's Maya?"

"She works in the clothing store."

"Oh, you mean the one you haven't worked at since you started helping out at the garage?"

"I have exams. I need to focus. Can't do both."

"Uh-huh. Well, that's great. I'm happy for you." Her voice lowered, and she lost her enthusiasm.

"Don't worry," I said, knowing exactly what she was thinking the moment she rubbed her hand across her chest. "I'm not leaving you."

"Promise."

"Would I lie?" I was going to hell. I'd done nothing but lie to her these last few weeks. But I wouldn't lie about us.

"No." She shook her head and smiled. "Where are we going?"

"Thought we could get some ice cream and maybe hang out at my house for a while. What do you think?"

"But, your dad?" Her voice was panicked. She'd never been to my house because I refused to bring her over when he was home. Actually, I refused to go back when he was there. I spent most nights driving around town, or at the shopping centre in Storm Cove until they kicked me out. I only went back when I knew he'd be asleep.

He'd been on my back more and more lately.

Chris was being released from rehab soon, and my father was worried I'd slip into my old ways. Not that he ever listened when I explained those drugs weren't mine. I'd taken them from Chris so he didn't do something stupid like OD in the school bathroom to get out of the trouble he'd found himself in.

My father only saw what he wanted to see, and he saw me as a failure. A major disappointment. All because he couldn't keep it in his pants and knocked up his secretary nineteen years ago.

Some things never changed.

"He's off screwing Sally somewhere."

Audrey's eyes widened. "Sally, the receptionist at school? That Sally?"

"Yeah. Caught them in his office yesterday."

"Oh, my god. Why didn't you tell me?"

"Because I really didn't want to think about it. It was a horrible image to get out of my head."

"Oh, that's so gross."

"You're telling me."

We were silent for a few moments.

"I'm excited to see your house." Audrey spun in her seat to face me, her eyes sparkling.

"Why?"

"Because I've never been there before."

"For good reason."

"I know. I don't want to hang around your dad any more than you do. So, this will be nice. Maybe Maya can come too?"

"Shit." I groaned and slapped my hand against the steering wheel. "I can't do it."

"What?"

157

"Lie."

"Lie about what?" She folded her arms and frowned at me.

I reached over and grabbed her hand. "My date. Everything. I'm sorry, bro. I haven't been completely honest."

Audrey gasped and began rocking back and forth. "You are going to leave, aren't you? I'm going to lose you."

"No, no. Of course not." I pulled the car into the parking lot out the front of the gelato shop by the beach. "Walk with me?"

Audrey gave a shaky nod. I got out of the car and helped her out too. She zipped her hoodie up and pulled the hood over her head, covering her face. The beach was empty, so she didn't need to worry, but it was still a public place, and her hood made her feel safe.

"I lied about my date. I don't have a date. I don't even know anyone called Maya." I laughed, surprised at the bitter tone in my own voice.

"Then, why?"

"Because I'm jealous as shit, bro. You said Christina had a date, and I hate the thought of her with someone else."

"But you said…"

"I know what I said, and I only said that because you are so damn adamant that you hate her, and I didn't want to upset you. She's really not like everyone thinks. I think she's changed. And, man, I just really want to screw her six ways from Sunday, you know?"

"Umm. No. No, I don't know. I don't

158

understand, Bennett. You can have any girl in the world. Why her?"

Any girl but the one standing in front of me. I pushed that thought aside as quickly as it came. We were friends. That was all it was and would ever be, and I was good with that.

"I don't know. We just work well together. And I've been trying to ignore her and the desperate need to bend her over her desk."

"Oh, my god. Stop. I don't want to hear it." Audrey blocked her ears, making me laugh.

"But I can't ignore her. So, when you said she had a date, I wanted to act like I didn't care. But I do care. Too much."

"I'm sorry, Bennett." We sat on a bench overlooking the beach.

"It's not your fault. It's mine."

"Why would you say that?"

I wrapped an arm around Audrey's shoulder when she shivered. It was a little cool so close to the water. "She's only dating him to get back at me for what I said."

"What did you say? Do I want to know?"

"I told her the truth."

"And that was?"

"That you will always come first. That she has to share me with you. That if anyone ever tries to force me to choose between you and them, I'd always choose you."

"You didn't?"

"I did. And I meant it. Like you said, whoever I'm with has to be okay with us, with this, and if they're not, then I want out."

159

"Bennett," Audrey groaned. "I'm sorry. I didn't mean for you to do that. I was just having a moment of weakness. I don't want you to risk any future relationships for me."

"Doesn't matter what you want. It is what it is. I told her the truth. You and I are a package deal, bro, and if someone tries to make me choose, they're not the right one for me."

Audrey gave me a watery smile.

"Don't cry."

"They're happy tears," she sniffed, "and sad ones too, because now I feel like I'm holding you back. You've been so good to me. But I feel like maybe I should let you go, as much as it hurts me."

"Nope. Not happening. We're tethered. Joined together. I'll get handcuffs if need be. You're not leaving me either, bro."

"Pink, fluffy ones?" she asked.

I narrowed my eyes. "Something you want to tell me, bro? Do you have pink, fluffy handcuffs I don't know about?"

Audrey cleared her throat and looked out to the water, completely ignoring my question, and I let it slide. Didn't want to embarrass her too much. "So, what are you going to do?"

"Wait and hope she comes to her senses."

CHAPTER NINETEEN

Christina

Three Weeks to go.

I tried. I tried my hardest to get Bennett out of my head. I even went on a date with Carter but couldn't for the life of me find anything remotely interesting about the guy. He bored me to tears. I guessed looks and personality were a hard package to come by.

Bennett was the perfect package.

I found myself watching him in class, taking in every detail, committing every smile—for Audrey—to memory, wishing I could run my hands through his hair, bite his lip, his collarbone. I looked for him in the halls, around Storm Cove. I checked my phone every three seconds hoping for a message from him. I was obsessed.

I hadn't spoken to him in weeks.

Exams were next week, and graduation was two

weeks after that.

Time was almost up, and I was still trying to work out whether I'd be okay with sharing his time and his affection with Audrey. It would be hard, take some getting used to. I was a jealous person by nature, and I didn't know how I would react if he ran out on me to go to her rescue. But I knew one thing.

I wanted Bennett Sawyer.

More than I wanted anything else. And I was willing to try.

I thought.

I poured myself a glass of wine and opened the curtains in my living room. The storm was raging outside, and I loved nothing more than watching the rain and the lightning. Deciding it was still warm enough that I could probably sit on my porch and watch the storm from my swing, I grabbed my book and my wine and made my way outside.

It was a beautiful night.

I grabbed the throw blanket and put it over my lap as I leaned back on the swing and got comfortable. Thunder boomed overhead, and the flash of lightning lit up my porch and illuminated a figure standing on the lawn in the rain.

I screamed.

Heavy footsteps thudded on my timber steps, and a thick, gravelly voice said, "Sorry."

I leaned forward and squinted in the dark at the tall, broad shape looming over me. "Bennett?"

"Yeah."

Pulling the blanket around my chin, I brought my knees to my chest. "What are you doing here?"

"Couldn't sleep." He shrugged as he stepped into the light coming through the window from the living room.

His eyes were dark, shoulders slumped, and he was dripping wet.

"Really?"

"No." He leaned against the weatherboards and kicked one black-booted foot up behind him on the wall.

Why did that look so sexy? My eyes travelled the length of his body. He was dressed head to toe in black, but it was the beanie on his head that really did things to me. No man should look that good in a woollen hat with a pom pom on top. It looked like a tea cosy, but he made it work.

"What, then?"

"Had a fight with my dad and didn't know where else to go."

"You had a fight with John, and you came here?" I tried to calm the stampede of raging wild animals in my stomach.

My mind was running a million miles an hour. He came to me.

"What about Audrey?" I asked tentatively as I stood from the swing and approached him slowly.

"I wanted to see you," he said, levelling me with a hard gaze.

Me. He wanted to see me. Not Audrey. He chose me over her.

And suddenly my decision was made.

I lunged for him. Ripped the beanie off his head and wound my fingers through his hair before pushing up on my toes, until my entire body was

163

pressed against his very firm, very cold, very wet one. I didn't care that he was dripping wet. All I wanted was his hands on my body and his lips on mine.

I kissed him. Long. Slow. Savouring every taste. Every touch.

Because I knew I had to stop before things got out of control.

I wanted him so much, and I only had to wait for three long, torturously painful weeks until I could do all the things I wanted to do to him. I pushed away, leaving us both gasping for breath.

"So, in three weeks?" Bennett quirked an eyebrow in question.

"It's on."

"Ahh, Ms. Brown. The things I've been imagining doing to you. Better prepare yourself."

"I'll be ready. Don't worry."

We stood on the porch staring at each other. The tension was thick, palpable, and if I didn't break it soon, all hope was lost.

"You should come inside and get dry. You'll get sick if you stay like that."

"Thanks." Bennett cleared his throat, kicked off his shoes, and followed me into the house.

"You know where the bathroom is. Go and have a shower, warm up, and I'll find you some dry clothes." I paused. "I think you still have a pair of track pants and a t-shirt here somewhere." That was a lie. I knew for a fact he still had clothes here. I knew that since I slept in his shirt most nights because my bed was so empty without him.

He smiled and dripped water all the way down

the hall and into my room. And I didn't mind one bit.

I laid his clothes out on the bed and fought the urge to peek through the crack in the bathroom door with every fibre in my body.

Three weeks.

I could last three weeks.

I'd already made it through seven.

The problem was now I'd kissed him twice, and it only served to increase my need for him. I had to keep it together, or I'd ruin any chance we had before it even began.

Bennett returned to the living room fifteen minutes later, freshly showered and smelling like strawberry shampoo. In fact, the shampoo smelt better in his hair than it did in mine. I handed him a glass of wine I'd poured while he was showering and made room on the sofa for him.

"You can stay until the storm eases," I said. I told myself I was doing the right thing. Being careful. Cautious. That it wasn't safe for him to drive in that weather, and I'd hate for anything to happen to him on the wet roads. Really, I just wanted his company.

He collapsed in the seat beside me and sighed.

"What was your fight about?"

"What?" Bennett looked at me. He must have been in his own world.

"With your dad. What was the fight?"

"He caught me talking to my friend Chris."

"Chris? And why is that a bad thing?"

"Chris got into trouble a couple years ago. Owed some people money, some other people drugs. They

165

were all after him, and the only way he could see of getting out if it was to kill himself. I found him at school with a bag of pills and a bottle of vodka. He was going to OD. So, I snatched the vodka off him and poured it out. Then I took the pills and threw them in my bag until I could flush them down the toilet."

"What happened?"

"I dropped my bag, and the pills fell out as a teacher walked past. I was expelled immediately. Dad was furious."

"But you were just looking out for your friend. You did the right thing."

"Dad didn't see it that way. He thought Chris got me hooked on drugs. And when I sold my car to pay Chris's debt, Dad flipped. Completely freaked out. Threatened to send me to live with my mother unless I cleaned up my act. I had no act to clean up but still had to follow his orders. I transferred to his school so he could keep an eye on me. Chris went to rehab and got sober. I paid his debts. So, Chris has got nothing to worry about now, but Dad still doesn't see it that way. He caught Chris and me talking tonight. We haven't seen each other for over a year. Dad came out, threatened to call the police if Chris didn't get off his property. Told me if I had anything to do with him again, he'd kick me out of the house. I told him if he did that, I'd expose all his dirty little secrets that he's been trying to keep quiet for nineteen years. And here we are."

"Bennett, I'm so sorry. Your dad's a prick."

Bennett laughed. "He is. But as soon as I graduate, I'm out. I'll find a job, study part-time, and get the hell out of his house."

"Sounds like a great plan." I took a sip of my wine and tried not to react to the way Bennett was looking at me. He managed to turn me into a puddle with just a glance.

"Can I ask you something?" he said after a while of silence.

"Sure."

"Tell me about what went down with Bailey and you in high school."

I gasped and stared at him with wide eyes. That was the last thing I expected him to ask.

"I mean, I get it if you don't want to talk about it. It's just I heard Bailey's version, and it doesn't paint you in a very good light."

"No, I guess it wouldn't. I was cruel back then." I sucked down more wine, needing to prepare myself for the conversation we were about to have. I'd never spoken about it to anyone.

"Yeah, I heard, which is why I want your story. Because I find it hard to believe you really were that much of a bitch."

I laughed. "I was. Indie used to call me Her Royal Whoreness behind my back. Totally deserved."

Bennett laughed. "She's creative. Still, it wasn't nice."

I poured Bennett another wine because he'd probably need it as well and then dived into my story.

"Neither was I, but in my defence, I was also incredibly naïve and lived a sheltered life. Privileged, but sheltered. I mean, you met my

167

father. My mother is just as bad. Growing up, Bailey and I were best friends. I loved the fact she basically worshipped the ground I walked on. Don't judge her on that. She moved around so much that she never felt truly comfortable anywhere or like she fit in. She latched on to me, and I abused that. I treated her like a doll. Talked her into dressing like me, wearing our hair the same, everything. It was a power trip. I did to her exactly what my mother did to me." I cradled my wine glass in my hand and shifted until my legs were folded under me.

"And then she began dating Chace, and I couldn't handle the fact that her attention was focused more on him. She was my friend. She idolised me…and Chace." I shook my head at the memories. "Everyone wore rose coloured glasses when it came to him, but I was the one who took the longest to see who he really was. He had me completely fooled for years. I was under his spell. And I loved him, even before he began dating Bailey. So, not only had I lost my best friend to a boy, I lost the boy I believed was the love of my life to my best friend. That's a lot for a fifteen-year-old to handle."

Bennett's hand slid over the sofa and found mine. His fingers twisted through mine, and I wanted nothing more than to close the distance between us and rest my head on his chest.

"As time wore on, I noticed Chace was getting more and more distant from Bailey. I mean, I noticed everything about him. Obsessed was an understatement. He changed his toothpaste, I noticed."

Bennett laughed but didn't say any more. He merely waited for me to continue. I couldn't see any judgement in his eyes, just genuine curiosity.

"I knew Bailey was a virgin. I was too. But I also knew she wanted to wait until it was absolutely right. I could sense Chace getting frustrated with her for making him wait. After all, he was a teenage boy. You know how they are."

Bennett nodded. "Horny all the fucking time."

I smiled.

"So, I tried to convince Chace to break up with her. Find someone better. Someone who was willing to sleep with him."

"You," Bennett said. It wasn't a question; it was understanding.

"I mean, I didn't want to hurt Bailey, but I loved Chace so much and honestly believed he should have been with me. All I wanted was my best friend back, her attention a hundred percent on me, and the boy of my dreams on *my* arm, not hers. I didn't think that was so much to ask. My intentions were good. I meant well. I just never thought through the consequences. Well, Chace refused to break up with Bailey. I saw red. Why didn't he want me? I'd give him everything he wanted and more if he gave me a chance."

I took a deep breath and sipped my wine.

"We were at a party one night. Bailey was home studying. She didn't party as much as everyone else. I saw Chace take a girl upstairs, and it hurt, you know? I felt like he was betraying me. It should have been me going upstairs with him, not someone else. And I know how bad that sounds, believe me.

169

But at the time, I didn't give Bailey a second thought. All I cared about was what his actions were doing to my feelings. I was jealous. So jealous. I stormed up the stairs and walked straight into that bedroom. Chace had the girl on the bed, and he was kissing her. She was mortified when she realised I was in there. I told her she had three seconds to get the hell out before I let the entire school know what she was about to do in that room. She bolted out the door so fast and never returned."

"What happened next?"

"Chace was pissed. He'd been trying to get in Bailey's pants for a year, and he'd finally given up hope and decided to just hook up with a random girl, and I ruined it. I was calm, collected, as I stepped into the room, closed the door, removed my clothes, and told him he could have me instead." I swallowed the lump in my throat as my stomach bubbled with sickness.

"I lost my virginity to Chace in a bedroom upstairs at a party while my best friend, his girlfriend, was at home studying. It didn't stop at the one time. It happened all the time, at every party, every time we went out anywhere Bailey didn't go. I didn't care, because I finally had the attention of the boy I loved. The boy I would do anything for. And because Chace was getting what he wanted from me, he spent more time hanging around me than he did with his girlfriend. So, that meant the less time Bailey spent with Chace, the more time she had to hang out with me. In my eyes, it was the way it was meant to be. I had my friend back, and I had the boy of my dreams sneaking out of my bedroom window every other night."

Bennett whistled and blinked a few times. "That's, uh…quite a story."

"That's only the beginning."

"There's more?"

"Well, that's the part Bailey doesn't know and can never know. I'll never forgive myself for how I was in high school. I know it is no excuse, but I was young, and only ever saw Chace. I wasn't used to not getting my way. At home, all I had to do was ask for something, and it was handed to me on a solid gold platter. And I'm sure you know the rest. How Chace broke up with her, and we made our relationship official after a couple of weeks."

"And how you caused her so much grief?" Bennett asked.

"It's going to sound crazy, but even though I had Chace, I was still jealous. It still didn't feel right. I lost my best friend because of him, and then to see her move on and be happy with Ryder and not miss me at all, it hurt. I wanted to make her suffer just a little of what I was suffering when I lost her."

"You lost her through your own actions."

"I know. I didn't say I made any sense in the way I thought back then."

"Thank you."

"For what?"

"Telling me why."

"Does it change your opinion of me?"

"No. I still don't think you're bad. A little misguided when you were younger, but not bad."

I groaned. "Where were you when I was seventeen?"

"Really want me to answer that?" He laughed.

"No, probably not. That's a little weird to think about."

CHAPTER TWENTY

Bennett

D-Day.

"Are you ready for this?" Audrey bounced down the stairs to me with a big smile on her face.

"No. Are you?" I frowned at her. She was terribly cheery, considering what the day entailed.

"Yes, actually. I feel great."

"What happened? What have you done to my Audrey?" I pinched her cheeks and made a show of examining her eyes and face.

"You're an idiot." She slapped my hands away and stood back to do a twirl. "Like?"

I took in her full appearance for the first time. And, shit. She was in a dress that exposed her chest and shoulders, her scars on full display for the entire world to see.

"You look beautiful."

"Thank you." She ducked her head and smiled shyly.

"What's the occasion?" I joked.

173

"You're not funny, Bennett."

"I'm hilarious."

"Annoying."

"Devastatingly good looking."

"Irritating."

"Charming."

"Painful."

I clutched my heart and winced. "Ouch, bro, that cut. Deep."

"You'll get over it. Now, are we going or not?"

"Don't you want to see me twirl?" I asked her with a frown.

"Go on, then." She rolled her eyes.

I spun around slowly on the spot so she could take in my appearance too.

"Well, what do you think?" I asked when I turned to face her.

"Eh…you scrub up all right. I guess," she said with a playful smile.

"All right? It took me forever to pick my outfit and get my hair just right. I look sexy."

"Your hair is in a bun, like always."

"What about the suit, Audrey?"

"The suit is nice," she deadpanned, and then she started giggling. "You look very handsome, Bennett. Now, can we go?"

"Where is everyone else?"

"They already left. We're going to be late."

"What are they going to do? Give us detention?"

"No, but they might not let us graduate."

My eyes widened. It was D-day. I had to graduate today. There was no other option. If I didn't, I might combust. Burst into flames.

"Let's go, then. Stop wasting time to admire my body."

"You're impossible."

"I'm endearing."

She groaned and grabbed my hand to drag me out the door. "Come on."

The school parking lot was full when we arrived. I had to circle around twice before I found a space because Ryder had stolen my spot at the front. When I complained about it to Audrey, she laughed.

"That was Ryder's spot when he was here. Guess he has first rights to it."

"We'll see about that."

I grabbed her purse out of the car and our gowns and caps from the back seat. "You didn't pack your hoodie?"

"I can't wear that thing with this dress. It'll look terrible, and Kenzie would kill me."

"But there's a lot of people here tonight."

"I know. But I have you, and Brody and the wolf pack will be in the audience. I'll be okay. I've hidden away for so long. Don't you think I should go out with a bang? It's our last time walking through these halls, Bennett. I want to do it with confidence."

I smiled at her and wrapped my arms around her waist, lifting her into the air and spinning us around until she laughed. "I'm so proud of you. Let's show them why we're together."

"We're not together."

"But they don't know that. Let me show you off."

"Okay." She linked her fingers through mine,

and we walked inside, me in my suit, and Audrey in her revealing black dress. She held her head high and tightened her grip on my hand. I could feel her trembling, but she walked with confidence and ease.

Fake it 'til you make it.

The whispers started almost immediately, and the stares followed us through the halls until we made our way to the gym. Audrey took a deep breath and smiled up at me.

"You did it. You okay?"

"Piece of cake." She winked, letting her shoulders relax when she realised the whispers weren't bad. No one was saying anything about her scars or calling her names. The whispers were out of shock and awe, admiration.

"Audrey, you look beautiful," Tina said.

"I love your dress."

"Wow, you look amazing."

Not one person looked at me, and that was more than okay. They were all mesmerised by the beautiful girl under my arm.

Audrey was doing great.

Christina walked into the room and announced, "We're starting in five minutes. Be ready." She approached us and smiled at Audrey. "You look lovely, Audrey."

Audrey gasped, her eyes wide with shock, and brushed her hand over her dress. "Thank you, Ms. Brown."

With a heated gaze in my direction, Christina turned and sauntered away. I followed the sway of her hips greedily with my eyes. Only a few more hours to go.

"Focus." Audrey slapped me on the chest.

"Sorry." We'd had a brief discussion about what today meant, other than graduation. And while Audrey still didn't understand why I wanted to bang our English teacher so bad, she was backing off and letting me make my own decisions, on the condition I didn't break her heart. Audrey's heart. Not Christina's. And that was the easiest promise to keep.

I placed her graduation gown over her shoulders and the cap on her head before doing the same with my own. One day, someone would design a nicer looking graduation gown. We looked like wizards in robes.

"All right, places, everyone," Christina called out, and we all moved into the gym to take our seats.

I walked Audrey to her seat, placed a kiss on her cheek, and said, "Good luck. I'll see you on the other side."

She smiled and nodded shakily. The nerves were creeping in. "You can do this," I whispered and walked off in search of my seat.

"Bennett." Christina approached.

"Ms. Brown, what can I do for you?" I smirked as she flushed pink.

"There's been a slight change to the schedule. Your name will be called immediately after Audrey."

"What? Why? It's alphabetical. She's D. I'm S."

"I'm well aware of that. I had the change made so you can be there with her if she needs you."

I smiled. The fact she did that proved she was

177

better than everyone gave her credit for. "You did?"

"Yes. I know how hard this must be for her to get up in front of the gym full of people and thought it would be best."

"Fuck. I really want to kiss you right now," I said quietly, my voice almost a growl.

"Later." Christina's eyes flashed with desire. "Go be with Audrey. She's going to need you."

"Thank you, Ms. Brown."

"You can thank me later."

"Oh, I'm going to thank you." I lowered my voice to a whisper. "All. Night. Long."

"Can't wait," she said with a serious expression before turning and walking away.

I ran back over to Audrey and took the seat beside her as she began rocking back and forth. "What are you doing here?"

"Ms. Brown put me on the schedule right after you. For support in case you needed it."

Audrey's head whipped around, and she sought out Christina. "Thank you," she mouthed, and Christina nodded with a smile.

"I can't believe she did that."

"Told you she wasn't so bad. You okay now?"

"Now that you're here, yes. Have you seen Brody yet? I can't find him." She craned her neck to look around the gym.

"Hang on." I climbed onto my seat so I could see over the crowds of people pouring in to watch us all graduate and spotted Brody, the Kellermans, Indie and Linc, Kenzie and Jeremy, Harper and Nate, Bailey and Ryder, Sage tucked against his chest a few rows behind the rest of the students. I reached down to Audrey and pulled her up onto her chair. "Here."

I pointed in the direction they were sitting.

"I can't see them," she said.

"I am not lifting you on my shoulders."

She frowned.

"They're there. Trust me."

"But I want to see."

"Fine."

I put my fingers in my mouth a whistled as loudly as I could. The entire gym fell silent and looked my way.

"Oh, my god, Bennett, everyone is looking."

"You want to see them, don't you?"

She nodded.

I turned back to face Brody, cupped my hand around my mouth, and shouted. "Hey, stand up."

Brody stood and blew a kiss at Audrey.

"And the rest of you," I called again.

One by one, they all stood and waved at Audrey, so she knew they were there.

"Mr. Sawyer, Miss Davide, please sit down." My father's voice boomed from the podium on the stage.

We quickly dropped into our seats and faced the front, trying not to laugh.

The ceremony started, and most of the first twenty minutes was my father talking shit. I swore he loved hearing the sound of his own voice. I didn't pay much attention; I was too focused on Audrey's bouncing knee beside me.

Leaning in close, I whispered, "Relax," and grabbed her hand. "We'll do it together."

They began calling the students' names, one by one, to come to the podium and collect their graduation certificate. The closer they got to Audrey's name, the more she bounced nervously beside me until my father's voice echoed through the speakers, "Audrey Davide."

Audrey froze. The bouncing knee no longer bounced. Her breaths became shallow, and panic marred her features.

"I'm right behind you," I reassured her, but she still didn't move.

My father called her name again, and I shot Christina a look that said "do something." She darted across the stage and whispered in my dad's ear. He nodded and surprised me by speaking again. "Audrey Davide and Bennett Sawyer."

I jumped out of my chair and held out my hand for Audrey. She was trembling, but with one arm around her waist and the other holding her palm to my chest, I led her to the stage and over to the podium to collect our certificates.

"Congratulations, Audrey." My father reached out to shake her hand, but she wouldn't remove it from my chest. I had to pry it away and place her hand in his.

"Congratulations, Bennett." He shook my hand and smiled at me, the first genuinely proud smile he'd ever given me. I nodded my thanks.

And then, doing the only thing I could do, I scooped Audrey up into my arms and spun her around as I had just done outside. "We did it, bro!"

Cheers and whistles echoed through the gym, and I turned Audrey to face the crowd, where the entire wolf pack were standing and clapping and shouting out congratulations to her.

She smiled and buried her head in her hands in embarrassment, and that only made them cheer louder. I picked her up again and ran off stage with her.

"You okay?" I asked once I'd set her down in her seat.

"Yeah, thank you. That was so embarrassing. I froze."

"You did amazing. I'm so proud of you," I reminded her.

We fell silent and watched the remainder of the ceremony. There were more speeches from the class captains and whoever graduated top of the class. I wasn't sure because all my attention was focused on my English teacher once again.

After it was finally over, I walked Audrey to her family, where they all congratulated her and showered her with hugs and kisses, before turning and doing the same to me. I had no one in that audience who cared, so I was touched by their gesture. They were great people.

"Now," Jeremy said, "the after party."

"There's an after party?" Audrey looked around.

"Of course. At the roadhouse. The whole class is invited," Indie answered.

"Why didn't I know about that?"

Kenzie laughed. "Surprise."

"Let's go and celebrate." Brody grabbed her hand and tugged her to the door.

I hesitated, wondering whether it would be a bad idea to drag Christina into the locker room and rip her dress off so soon.

"Bennett, hurry up!" Audrey called over her shoulder, making my decision for me.

She wanted me at the after party. So, Christina would have to wait.

CHAPTER TWENTY-ONE

Christina

My steps were slow, controlled, as I walked toward the roadhouse, but my breaths were heavy, laboured with anticipation of what was to come later that night.

The countdown was over. Bennett was officially no longer my student.

Sure, we could wait until the dust settled, but I had waited long enough.

Ten weeks was too long.

The music echoed through the parking lot, and the neon sign above the diner cast a purple glow over everything.

Ten minutes was all the time I was giving myself in there because I knew who was there and was sure none of them wanted to see me. Besides, students didn't want to hang around with the teachers, anyway, with the exception of one student in

183

particular.

Bennett caught my attention the instant I walked through the doors and began weaving his way through the crowd to me.

"Bennett." I smiled, still trying to act cool.

"Ms. Brown. Glad you could make it."

"Oh, I'm not staying long. Just popped in for a moment, and then I'm out."

"Oh." He folded his arms across his chest and grinned. "Big plans?"

"You could say that."

We stood there staring at each other, sharing secret smiles, knowing exactly what was going to happen the second I walked out those doors.

"Well, be sure to say goodbye before you leave," Bennett said.

"I will."

Bennett sauntered away, leaving me staring after him pathetically, and I didn't care.

"Christina," a voice said behind me. Taking a breath, I turned slowly on the spot to see Indie scowling at me. "What are you doing here?"

"I'm a teacher. I'm supposed to be here."

"I don't like it."

"You don't have to. I've spoken with Bailey, and we've decided to move on and leave the past in the past. I'm not here to cause any trouble, Indie, I swear."

"If I find out that—"

"I know. You think Ryder hasn't given me that same speech? Or Jeremy? If I screw up, you'll make my life hell."

"I was going to say kill you with a smile, but

184

whatever. Long as you know." She turned and stomped away toward a guy who looked like he'd just stepped out of the surf, with his blond dreadlocks tied on top of his head. Must be Linc, her fiancé. I remembered how obsessed she was with him in high school.

I stood awkwardly in the middle of the dancefloor and contemplated leaving—I did have much more important matters to attend to—when Bailey waved me over.

"Hi," I said as I approached cautiously.

"Would you like to join us?" She smiled. One look at her group of friends told me I was absolutely not welcome to sit with them.

"Umm…" I looked for an excuse. Anything to get away from there. Bailey was fine on her own. Ryder, I could deal with. But the stares from Kenzie and Indie were impossible to ignore.

Audrey rushed over to the table. Her cheeks were flushed, and she was out of breath.

"You need to take it easy, cupcake," a guy with dark hair said as he pulled her to him. She draped her arm around his shoulders.

"Dance with me?" she asked him as she bounced on the tips of her toes excitedly. I'd never seen her this way, so happy and carefree. She was relaxed and beautiful when she smiled. I could understand at that moment why Bennett was enamoured with her.

"Bennett was doing a pretty good job at that," the guy said and pressed a kiss to her lips. He must have been Brody, her older boyfriend.

Audrey giggled. "Yeah, he was great. Did you

see him dip me?"

"I did." Brody smiled, and I was amazed that he was so calm and at ease with how close she and Bennett were. "Why don't you go back out there?"

"I can't," she said and flicked her gaze to me. "Bennett just left."

"What? Why?" Indie asked.

Audrey shrugged. "Said something very important came up and…" She looked at me again, and I got the feeling she was subtly trying to give me a message, but that would mean she knew about Bennett and me, and that she had probably known the entire time. "He couldn't wait any longer, or things would get explosively messy." She screwed up her face in disgust, and I chuckled.

"What could be so important that he had to leave his own graduation early? And leave you behind?" Indie frowned.

"A chick," Ryder and Linc answered.

"What?" Bailey asked with wide eyes.

Kenzie laughed. "He's getting laid."

"About fucking time." Ryder adjusted the little pink bundle in his arms.

"You're telling me. You haven't had to work with him as much. Never seen a guy so wound up." Jeremy, Kenzie's boyfriend, nodded in agreement.

"So, Christina, you want to join us?"

"No, I need to go. I only stopped by for a minute. No one wants their teacher around, anyway."

"Okay, next time, then." Bailey smiled. Why was she so nice?

"Sure. Congrats again, Audrey."

"Thanks, Ms. Brown." She waved. A look

passed between us, and I was sure she was trying to tell me something, but I couldn't decipher it.

I rushed out to my car, noticing that Bennett's was long gone. I assumed he would go to my place, but who really knew.

I pulled my phone out of my bag to text him when I saw I already had one waiting from him.

Bennett: Did you get my message?

Christina: Your very subtle one from Audrey. Yes. I'm on my way.

Bennett: Drive safe. Looks like it's going to rain.

Christina: Aww, you care.

Bennett: I've waited ten weeks for this, Ms. Brown. I can't wait any longer if you run your car off the road.

Bennett: Yes, I care.

Christina: See you soon.

I climbed in my car and took off toward Storm Cove.

Bennett was right. The rain started about halfway home, and by the time I pulled my car into the garage at the back of my house, it was bucketing down. I got out and stood at the edge of the garage, contemplating running across my back yard. Trust me to pick a house with a detached garage.

But then I saw Bennett standing on the bottom step in the rain.

Without giving another thought to the water pouring down around us, I ran over to him.

He met me in the middle of the yard. "What are you doing in the rain?"

"Don't know, really. Just wanted to feel it on my face." He tilted his face back and looked up at the sky.

I did the same thing and laughed. I felt so carefree and light right at that moment.

"We're saturated," I said, looking at him.

"I know."

He wrapped his arms around my waist and pulled my body flush against his. The cold from our wet clothes, mixed with the warmth of our bodies, was a wonderful feeling.

"Hi," he whispered, dragging his nose along mine.

"Hi." My hands threaded through his hair, and I pushed up on my toes to try to get closer to him.

Bennett's fingers dusted over my exposed collarbones, my dress no longer hiding a lot, thanks to the rain, and down my chest, skimming over my breasts and across my ribs. They continued their slow movements until he grabbed my thighs and wrapped them around his waist.

"We should get inside out of the rain," I said.

"Why? We're already wet. A little more water won't hurt."

He had a point, but I had different ideas for what we could do inside other than drying off.

Bennett's lips found my neck as he held me close, making their way slowly up my throat until, finally, after what felt like a lifetime, he kissed me.

Slow. Deep.

I savoured every moment. Every flick of his tongue against mine. Every stolen breath.

My body trembled from his lips alone, and I wanted him right there in my back yard. But that was crazy, right?

This moment, the build-up, the anticipation, nothing could have prepared me for the onslaught of feelings I was having for this man. This beautiful, handsome man, who came into my life when I needed him most and stayed, waited until now.

His mouth and hands worked together to torture me slowly. His hips moved against mine, and I couldn't take it anymore. It had been too long since I last felt his arms around me. Too long since he last kissed me with so much enthusiasm and passion. Too long since I felt his skin against mine.

"Bennett," I gasped as one of his hands worked its way under my dress.

"Yes, Ms. Brown?"

"No more screwing around. Ten weeks was long enough. What are you waiting for?"

"Just enjoying the moment." His hand slid further under my dress, and my eyes rolled back. "Just enjoying the moment." He skimmed his teeth across my collarbone.

"There will be plenty more moments, trust me." I gasped. "I need you now."

"Yes, Ms. Brown." I almost exploded just hearing him say my name. It was such a turn-on.

Bennett held me closer as he walked up the stairs and onto my back patio, but he didn't go inside.

"Where are you going?"

"Right here," he breathed against my lips and set me down on my outdoor lounge. The fabric was cold and wet against my already soaked skin.

"Door is right there." I pointed as he dropped to his knees in front of me.

"But the rain is romantic," he said and kissed the tops of my knees, then proceeded to trail his hands down my legs to the straps of my heels.

"Hmmm. I think these can stay."

"My shoes?" I was still stuck on the romance part. He wanted romance? I thought it was going to be so far from romantic. Rough. Fast. Hard. Anything but romantic. But I was okay with romance. Really, really okay if he kept looking at me the way he was.

"I've been having fantasies about them all term, Ms. Brown." He placed a kiss on the inside of my ankle then stood and grinned.

Ovaries exploded.

His fingers worked the buttons on his shirt, but he wasn't fast enough. I climbed to my feet and helped him peel his shirt off at an excruciatingly slow pace. Next was his belt, then the button on his pants, and finally the zip. When he was standing in front of me in nothing but his boxers, I leaned in and licked drops of water from his chest. My tongue twisted and swirled, tasting his skin.

Bennett's fingers dipped down and grasped the bottom of my dress before he pulled it over my head, leaving us both in our underwear.

This moment would change everything.

This was the moment we'd anticipated for ten weeks.

This moment was epic.

This moment was just the beginning.

I unclasped my bra, never taking my eyes off Bennett, while he removed his boxers. Finally, his fingers tore at the flimsy material of my panties, and they fell to the ground.

His hands dug into my hips, and he fell back onto the lounge, pulling me down on top of him and hissing when the cold, wet fabric connected with his skin.

He kissed me, his tongue exploring my mouth while his fingers traced light patterns over my skin. The rain still poured down over us, but it was a welcome relief to the heat I was experiencing everywhere. His touch was scorching, searing itself onto my soul, never to be erased. That was it. He was a part of me now, and I was never letting go.

Bennett reached down and pulled a condom from his pants, never once removing his mouth from mine. Lifting me by the waist, he shifted me into place and moved his hips up into mine.

He groaned.

I moaned.

We moved together perfectly.

Every touch, every sensation, multiplied by a thousand. It was perfect bliss. Meant to be. His hands explored my body, his tongue tasted my skin, and all I could do was enjoy every moment, until it was too much to bear and I saw stars, fireworks, Bennett's smile.

I collapsed against his chest, absolutely spent. His fingers traced my back gently, and he whispered in my ear, "Worth the wait."

"Definitely." I pressed my lips to his and rolled my hips again.

"Can we go inside now?" he asked, brushing a wet strand of hair out of my face.

"I thought the rain was romantic?" I shifted my hips again, smiling when he groaned and bit my collarbone.

"It was. But now it's fucking freezing, and my balls are about to drop off. What would we do then?"

That was enough for me. I climbed off his lap and ran inside, dripping water all the way down the hall, through my bedroom, and into my bathroom, where I began to run a hot bath.

"I like the way you think, Christina." Bennett's eyes darkened as he crossed the threshold and scooped me into his arms, stepping into the bath in one smooth movement.

"It's Ms. Brown to you." I smirked.

"Anything you say."

CHAPTER
TWENTY-TWO

Bennett

Three weeks after D-Day.

Jeremy slid a beer across the bar to me.

"Thanks, man." I'd had a long day, and a cold beer was the next best thing to dragging Christina to bed.

Three weeks, and things hadn't eased off. I spent nearly every night at her place, and every minute I wasn't at work or with Audrey, as well. We were definitely making up for lost time.

"So…spill," Ryder said from beside me.

"What?" I took a swig of beer. The cool, bitter liquid was refreshing after a long day working in the heat of the garage.

My phone buzzed on the bar with a text message.

Christina: Can I leave yet?

I smiled. I could picture her face. She was currently sitting at Bailey's house with Audrey and the rest of the girls. Bailey had organised an afternoon tea or some crap and banned the guys, which was why they were all here staring at me and waiting for me to answer a question I didn't know the answer to.

"What, he asks as he smiles goofily at his phone." Linc laughed.

Bennett: No. I'm sick of hiding this.

"I'm not smiling goofily at my phone."

Christina: But...

"Who is she?" Brody asked.
"She, who?"
"The chick you're messaging." Nate slapped me on the back of my head. These guys gossiped worse than girls sometimes.

Bennett: We need to tell everyone.

"Don't know who you're talking about."
Here I was, flat out lying to them, and at the same time convincing Christina she has to tell the girls about our relationship. It really would be so much easier if they all knew, not that I minded sneaking around. That was kind of fun. The risk of getting caught with my pants down, literally, was exhilarating. But I hated putting Audrey on the spot and having her lie for us. It wasn't her secret to

keep, and I didn't want to do that to her.

Jeremy scoffed. "The chick who has put a stupid smile on your face since the day you graduated."

"You trying to say I was miserable before?"

"You were a moody bitch. Lucky I didn't fire you."

Christina: Well, have you told the guys yet?

Bennett: No.

But in my defence, I had no one here to support me. Christina had Audrey's support, and I was left alone to tell the alpha wolves that I was banging the chick they all despised. In an odd turn of events, Audrey and Christina started to get along really well. There was no tension or weirdness between them at all, and Audrey even admitted she may have been wrong about Christina, and maybe, just maybe she might have changed.

Audrey wasn't the only one to see it either. Bailey had too, and that was why Christina had been invited to her girly afternoon tea party or whatever it was they were doing. I thought Audrey mentioned something about books. A book club, maybe? And we all knew that was code for wine club.

Christina: You better make this up to me.

Bennett: I have a few ideas ;)

"I know who it is," Ryder announced.

Of course, he fucking did. I was not at all surprised. He was the most perceptive person I'd ever met, and he saw things in places where there was nothing to see. He knew things before anyone else did.

"You do?" I raised an eyebrow at him, kind of hoping he didn't know, but at the same time really wishing he did so he could out me to everyone. It would be easier coming from him.

"About this high." He gestured with his hand Christina's rough height. "Blonde. Red lips. Am I getting warmer?"

I groaned and tilted my head back. "How long have you known?"

He shrugged. "Graduation."

"What?"

"It was obvious."

"What was obvious?" Linc asked, looking between us.

"Apparently, only to you," I said and took another mouthful of beer.

"What are we missing?" Nate asked.

"Bennett, here, is screwing his English teacher." Ryder nodded.

"Bailey?" Linc stared with wide eyes.

"Bailey's not blonde, dickhead."

"Well, then, who…? Oh! No way! Christina, really?"

I shrugged and grinned. "Yeah."

"Why?"

"Nipple clamps," was my response, causing Nate to choke on the mouthful of beer he'd just taken, spitting amber liquid all over the bar.

"Seriously?" Brody's eyebrows lifted.

"Offered to lend them to Audrey, but she punched me and called me a weirdo."

The guys laughed.

"But Christina?" Nate asked seriously.

"Yep."

Jeremy grabbed a cloth and wiped the beer Nate had spat everywhere. "Since when?"

"Well, we kind of hooked up last school holidays."

"You slept with your English teacher?" Linc threw his head back and laughed. "And I thought our relationships were all screwed up and not normal. But that's crazy."

He was right. In theory, all their relationships weren't exactly traditional, and they all crossed some sort of moral line.

"We called it off the moment we realised she was my teacher."

"So, no quickies in the janitor's closet?" Jeremy leaned on the bar.

"No. Nothing all term to graduation."

"Why didn't you say anything?" Brody asked.

"Because I know how everyone feels about her."

They all fell silent because they knew I was right. No one liked her except Audrey and Bailey, and no one wanted to give her a chance.

"Sorry, man. Look, it's your life. It might just take some getting used to having her around as well," Ryder said. "For whatever reason, you, Bailey, and Audrey see something that we're all missing. We just have to trust your judgement."

"Yeah?"

197

"Yeah." He nodded.

I looked at Jeremy, and he shrugged. Brody and Nate nodded in agreement with Ryder. And Linc…he was pinching his nipples.

"Dude?" Nate elbowed him. "You better not be thinking what I think you're thinking."

"What?" Linc dropped his hands and widened his eyes innocently.

"No nipple clamps."

"But…" Linc rubbed his chest.

Nate groaned and covered his eyes. "Indie is my sister. No nipple clamps."

"Right." Linc laughed, and I couldn't help but laugh too. Nate looked mortified.

We all looked up as the door to the bar opened, effectively ending our conversation as the girls all walked in.

"What are you doing here?" I wrapped an arm around Audrey's shoulders and kissed her head before spinning her into Brody's waiting arms. You'd be forgiven for thinking it was a move we'd practiced, but we hadn't. It was simply a natural progression in our weird friendship.

"Book club ended."

"You ran out of wine, didn't you?" Ryder asked Bailey as he pulled her in for a kiss.

Kenzie scaled the bar and jumped behind it with Jeremy. Indie was whispering to Linc, who was wiggling his eyebrows at her while holding her hands on his chest, leaving me no doubt that he was talking about nipple clamps. I snorted.

Harper moved over to sit beside Nate, leaving Christina standing there alone, twisting her fingers uncomfortably. She flicked her gazed to me before darting her gaze around at everyone.

"Ms. Brown." I stood and approached her. She gasped as I reached for her hips and pulled her to me, before lowering my head and capturing her lips in a searing kiss that had Audrey groaning and everyone else making crude comments. But I didn't care. They all knew about us, and they accepted it.

Things were looking up.

EPILOGUE

Christina

I paced my living room and looked at my watch. Where was he? He was never late. And tonight wasn't a night I could afford to be late. Tonight was important, probably one of the most critical moments of my life, and Bennett wasn't here yet.

I walked into my kitchen and poured another glass of wine, hoping it would calm my nerves. The liquid warmed my throat and my belly, yet I was still trembling. What if it was a disaster?

What if I said the wrong thing?

What if I was asked a question I couldn't answer?

I knew there'd be many.

Where was Bennett?

I checked my phone for a text or missed call from him and found nothing. Pressing his name, I bought my phone to my ear and listened to the dial tone.

"Ms. Brown?" His deep, velvety voice was

smooth and sexy when he answered the phone. Almost a purr.

I melted. Still, after two months of hiding out in my house in very little clothes, in my bed, my back yard—that was becoming a regular occurrence—hearing him call me Ms. Brown did things to me, my body. Would it ever stop? I hoped it didn't. The butterflies he used to give me were nothing compared to the whirlpool I felt now.

I got giddy just thinking about him. I loved his smile. The dimples that dented his cheek when he laughed. The way his blue eyes shone with delight and darkened to a stormy blue with pleasure. The way he wrapped his arm around me and held me close while we slept. The way he cooked breakfast shirtless. The way his hair fell in his face when it wasn't tied up. The way his tongue peeked out the corner of his mouth when he was concentrating.

"Where are you?"

"Uhhh…about that. I've been held up. I'm not sure when I'm going to make it."

I looked down at my dress, the one I'd bought specially for this night, and frowned. "What's happened?"

"I can't really talk about it right now."

"Everything okay?"

"Not sure yet. You can go without me. I'll meet you there when I finish dealing with this shit."

"Are you crazy? No way! I'm not going alone."

"Then what do you want to do?"

"I'll wait for you, unless you think it's going to take too long, then you call and cancel."

"We don't need to cancel. There's no RSVP or

reservation or anything, Christina. It's the Kellermans."

I know, but..." I took a deep breath. "They're expecting us, and I don't want to make a bad impression by being late or by not informing them we can't make it."

"Bad impression, huh?"

"Yes, I want them to like me, Bennett. I do. I was horrible in the past, and they're all finally coming to terms with us, largely thanks to Audrey and Bailey, and I want to make things right. Not showing to dinner would not be in our best interests."

"Ours? How'd I get roped into this?"

"Yep. We're an 'our' now. I've decided."

"Oh, you've decided. Do I get a say in this?" His tone was teasing and playful.

"No."

"So demanding, Ms. Brown. Lucky I love a woman who knows what she wants."

"Love?"

"What?'

"You said love."

"No, I didn't. You said love."

"Pretty sure you—"

"Okay. Fine. Whatever. Maybe I did. Sort of. A little bit."

"Does that mean—?"

"Jesus, Ms. Brown. You're a hard-ass tonight. Yes, maybe I do. Sort of. A little bit." The phone went silent except for Bennett's shaky breath. I smiled, feeling that stampede getting more furious. My heart was pounding against my rib cage so hard

I could feel it in my throat.

"Bennett?" I said.

He groaned, and I could imagine him right then. Eyes closed, face screwed up, fingers pinching the bridge of his nose as he tilted his head back.

"I maybe, sort of, a little bit..." I trailed off.

"Yes?" His voice was low, unsure.

Was it wrong that I wanted to mess with him a little bit? Maybe. He never got nervous. He was the most confident person I'd ever met, but right then I could hear it in his breath, and the tremor in his voice.

"Love you too," I whispered.

"Fuck," he hissed.

"What?"

"You had to say that now?"

My stomach sank. Did he not mean he loved me when he said it earlier? Maybe I just screwed everything up. What if I was the only one invested in this relationship, and he thought it was nothing more than sex? Really, really great sex. "Ummm, I can take it back if you'd prefer."

"Don't you fucking dare. But now how am I meant to deal with my father and him trying to kick me out..."

"What?" John was trying to kick him out. The guy was a piece of shit, and I wanted nothing more than to air his dirty laundry all over town, let everyone know what a pathetic excuse for a human being he was. But I learned my lesson the hard way. I wasn't that girl anymore. I didn't want to be that girl. I wanted to be the girl worthy of Bennett's love.

"Doesn't matter. But I can't concentrate on that when all I want to do is come home to you and hear you say it again."

A grin spread across my face, so wide my cheeks hurt. "I love you."

"Again?"

"I love you."

"Again?"

"Come on, Bennett, really?"

"Yes, really. No one other than Audrey has ever fucking told me they loved me."

My heart clenched, and pain shot through me at the little piece of information. Another reason to hate his parents. "I. Love. You."

"I have to call Audrey."

"What? You're kidding, right? Now?"

"Yes. Now. I have to cancel on dinner so I can come to your place and make you scream 'I love you, Bennett' so loud the neighbours complain. Over. And over again."

"That confident in your abilities, huh?"

"You bet."

"Okay, fine. Go and call Audrey. Get your video chat out of the way now, so there are no interruptions later. I'll be here. Waiting. With the silk scarf and…"

"Nipple clamps?" Excitement laced his voice, and I could picture his eyes sparkling and getting darker as he thought about the night ahead.

"Uh-huh."

"Knew there was a reason I loved you."

I laughed. "And, Bennett, pack a suitcase. All your clothes and important stuff."

"Why?"

"Move in with me?"

"I can't move in with my English teacher after only two months. What would people think?"

"You slept with her the day you met her…"

"Touché."

"I'll see you soon."

"Are we really doing this?"

"Do you want to live on the street? Or worse, continue living with your father?"

"Hell, no!"

"Then we're really doing it."

"Damn straight, we're doing it. All night long. Better find your ruler, Ms. Brown." He laughed and ended the call.

Was I sorry we were going to miss dinner at the Kellermans'? No. Not at all. They did it every week. We could try again next week. If we ever left my bed.

Crap.

It all happened so fast. I hadn't even thought it through properly, but Bennett was about to move into my house. With me. Because he loved me. And I loved him.

Oh, my god.

I needed more wine.

It was a huge commitment.

A giant step.

But I was willing to take it. The more I thought about it, the more I realised I'd never want anyone else. It was him. Only him.

I went to my room, soon to be our room, and changed out of my dress into something a little less comfortable, a lot more revealing, before returning to the living room and waiting for Bennett to come home.

My body was alight with anticipation. The excitement I felt was akin to the night of his graduation. Intense. Strong. Undeniable.

And then my phone rang. Not recognising the number, I thought about ignoring it, but something told me not to.

"Hello?"

"Hey, whore face," a man's cheery voice greeted. There was only one person who called me that, and I couldn't blame him, as much as it hurt to hear. We hadn't spoken to or seen each other in a few years. "It's Jack."

"I know. I remember."

"Of course, you do. I'm unforgettable."

He wasn't wrong.

I sighed and closed my eyes, preparing myself for his answer to my next question. "How'd you get my number?"

"I know a person, who knows a person, who knows a person, who heads the Royal Whoreness committee, who gave me your number."

"You're an asshole." I was tempted to hang up. I would not let Jack dampen my mood.

"Jack-ass actually. Ask Lincoln."

"Is there a reason for your call? Or did you just ring to insult me?"

"There's a reason. The insults are just an added bonus. I need your help."

He needed my help. And he actually thought I'd help him after the names he'd just called me.

"What makes you think I want to help you?"

"Oh, whore face, you will when you find out what it is I need help with. Or rather *who* I need help with."

"Who or what do you need help with?"

"Chace."

Oh, Fuck.

ACKNOWLEDGEMENTS

I'd like to thank Limitless Publishing for sticking with this series and continuing to publish my work. It wouldn't have been possible without you.

My family, again, for putting up with my erratic schedule and allowing the time and peace to write when I needed it most. You guys are the best.

Lori, for polishing my manuscript and making it shine and sparkle and be the best it can be.

Deranged Doctor Design for yet another gorgeous cover. Seriously, they get better and better with each one you create for me. Thanks for the promotional and marketing materials you've designed as well. You nail it every time.

Amber, you're a legend, and I couldn't do all the other stuff on top of the writing without you. You're always there when I need you.

My extra pairs of eyes—you know who you are. Without your eyes, I'd never catch any errors in the manuscript because mine clearly don't work as well as I think they do.

My street team for sharing and pimping my stuff out, and for being there when I need to bounce ideas or just can't make a decision. You help in so many ways.

Fiona. Again. Always. Because you are with me every step of the way. And WAFFLES. ;-)

And lastly…my beautiful readers and my reader group. You are the most important. Each and every one of you who have read one of my books or all of them, thank you. I couldn't do it without you. You guys are seriously amazing, and I'm so grateful for you all and the support you give me, the encouragement, and your excitement for my books.

About the Author

R. Linda drinks wine and writes books.

A coffee-addicted, tattoo-enthusiastic fangirl with a slight obsession for a particular British boy band and solo artist, she is a writer of Contemporary YA/NA Romance and Suspense, sometimes dabbling in Paranormal as well.

Renee lives in Melbourne, Australia, with her husband and two sons. When not writing, she can often be found reading books to her children and cuddling up with them on the couch to watch their favourite movies.

Connect with R. Linda:

Facebook:
https://www.facebook.com/rlindanovels/

Instagram:
https://www.instagram.com/rlindaauthor

Twitter:
https://www.twitter.com/rlindawrites

Website:
https://www.rlindanovels.com

Pinterest:
https://www.pinterest.com/abookishdelight

Get up close and personal with R. Linda along with some sneak peeks and exclusive giveaways and more in her reader group.

Reader Group:
https://www.facebook.com/groups/340494186367286/

Never miss an update. Get a free short story when you subscribe to my newsletter.
https://www.rlindanovels.com/subscribe

Be sure to sign up for my monthly newsletter to stay up to date on all upcoming releases, sales, giveaways, and more.
https://www.rlindanovels.com/subscribe

Join our Reader Group on Facebook and don't miss out on meeting our authors and entering epic giveaways!

Limitless Reading

Where reading a book
is your first step to becoming
limitless...

LIMITLESS PUBLISHING *Reader Group*

Join today! *"Where reading a book is your first step to becoming limitless..."*

https://www.facebook.com/groups/LimitlessReading/